OCT 1987

11/87

adult

# A Justice
## for All the People

The United States Supreme Court in 1916, shortly after Brandeis, *standing*, *far left*, was appointed COLLECTION OF THE
SUPREME COURT OF THE UNITED STATES

JEWISH BIOGRAPHY SERIES

# A Justice for All the People
## LOUIS D. BRANDEIS

BY DAVID C. GROSS

*illustrated with photographs*

LODESTAR BOOKS   E. P. DUTTON   NEW YORK

The quotations at the beginning of chapters
are by Justice Brandeis.

*Library of Congress Cataloging in Publication Data*

Gross, David C., date.
  A justice for all the people.

  (Jewish biography series)
  Includes index.
  Summary: A biography of the lawyer, judge, popularizer
of Zionist causes, and first Jew to serve on the Supreme
Court, who helped end child labor in America, introduced
the concepts of social security, minimum-wage laws, and
unemployment compensation, and, in short, devoted his
life to social justice.
  1. Brandeis, Louis Dembitz, 1856–1941—Juvenile
literature.  2. Judges—United States—Biography—
Juvenile literature.  [1. Brandeis, Louis Dembitz,
1856–1941. 2. Judges. 3. Jews—Biography] I. Title.
II. Series.
KF8745.B67G76  1987  347.73'2634  [B]  86-21454
ISBN 0-525-67194-3  347.3073534  [B]  [92]

Published in the United States by E. P. Dutton,
2 Park Avenue, New York, N.Y. 10016,
a division of NAL Penguin Inc.

Published simultaneously in Canada by
Fitzhenry & Whiteside Limited, Toronto

Editor: Virginia Buckley

Printed in the U.S.A.    W    First Edition
10 9 8 7 6 5 4 3 2 1

for Eric and Neil

# CONTENTS

# ACKNOWLEDGMENTS

I am happy to express my thanks to Justice Brandeis's grandson Frank Gilbert for his helpfulness. The public relations department of Brandeis University and the Zionist Library and Archives in New York have also been cooperative in supplying information and data.

And a special note of thanks is due to Virginia Buckley, my editor, who waited patiently for the manuscript to unfold from my typewriter.

DAVID C. GROSS

# A MAN CALLED BRANDEIS

Although many people have heard of Louis D. Brandeis, few people know how great a man he really was. Among the many organizations named for him are a major university in Waltham, Massachusetts; a modern Jewish day school on Long Island; chapters of various Jewish organizations; and a kibbutz (farming collective) in Israel called *Ein Ha-shofet*, "Well of the Judge."

And yet, in the first fifty years of his long life, he was hardly a member of the Jewish community. He was never a Bar Mitzvah, and when he married, the ceremony was not conducted by a rabbi. The only times he entered a synagogue were to deliver speeches in support of Zionism, the movement to reestablish a Jewish homeland in Palestine for hundreds of thousands of oppressed Jews.

He was the first Jew to serve as a justice of the United States Supreme Court, the highest court in the land, a position he filled from 1916 to 1939 with distinction. President Franklin D. Roosevelt spoke of him as the prophet Isaiah of biblical times.

During his lifetime, he helped make the Zionist cause popular among Jews and Gentiles. As a lawyer and later as a judge, he fought hard to improve the living conditions of all people. He helped put an end to child labor in America and introduced the concepts of social security, minimum-wage laws, and unemployment compensation. He wanted big business to deal fairly with labor, and he wanted the national government to share its powers with the states.

Like the prophets of old, he preached the highest possible moral standards. He devoted his life to making his noble ideals become a living reality in the country he loved so much.

# A Justice
## for All the People

I have only one life, and it is short enough. Why waste it on things I don't want most? I don't want money or property most. I want to be free.

—LOUIS D. BRANDEIS

# 1

## *Louisville*

*Education must continue throughout life.*

When Louis David Brandeis was nearly seven years old, in the year 1863, he helped his mother hand out coffee and biscuits to Union soldiers passing through his hometown, Louisville, Kentucky, on their way to the great Civil War battles that were raging in the South.

Abraham Lincoln was president, and the war had divided the young American nation into two sides—the North, whose citizens wanted to put an end to slavery, and the South, whose citizens wished to set up their own country, to be called the Confederacy, where slavery would continue.

All the members of the Brandeis family were in favor of abolition, which meant they wanted to put an end to slavery. The idea of one group of people enslaving another group went against everything that the Brandeis family believed in. Louis's parents, Adolph and Frederika, had fled their

3

home in Bohemia (in Czechoslovakia) because of oppression and had traveled thousands of miles to their new nation to live as free people.

In the same year, President Lincoln had issued the Emancipation Proclamation, which declared that America could no longer allow slavery to exist in the rebellious states. Louis did not understand all the words in Lincoln's famous statement, but he knew that Lincoln was ready to fight for justice and equality for all—and this was the beginning of his own lifelong wish to do the same thing.

Two years later the Civil War ended, and slavery in the United States was abolished. The Southern states remained in the United States. When Lincoln was assassinated, Louis cried bitterly. He had loved and admired the president. Although Louis was only nine years old, he had already made up his mind that somehow he would follow in the footsteps of the president.

Louis was the son of immigrants to America who had left their home in Europe in search of a new life where freedom for all people was a right guaranteed by the American Constitution. The Brandeis family took every word in the Declaration of Independence and in the Constitution very seriously. America's determination to provide each American with life, liberty, and the pursuit of happiness became, for Louis, a lifelong motto—and a goal that had to be reached.

Louis's father was born in Prague of an old Jewish family that could trace its beginnings in that part of Europe to the fifteenth century. As a young man he wanted to become a chemist but had to settle for agriculture, which he studied in the local technical school. Although he was graduated with honors, Adolph could not find a job. Times were hard for people in Prague and Bohemia in 1843, especially for Jews, who were not allowed to work as freely as Gentiles.

In the meanwhile, Adolph had fallen in love with Frederika Dembitz and wanted to get married. Without a job and without a promising future, he began to think of far-off America, where, according to everything he had heard, there was opportunity and freedom for all. In 1848, revolutions swept over central Europe, and young Adolph and Frederika worried about their future. They were afraid that sooner or later the Jews would be made to suffer for the economic and political unrest that was certain to come.

Three families—the Brandeises, the Dembitzes, and the Wehles (the family of Frederika's mother)—decided to send Adolph to America, to find out if emigrating to the United States was a good idea. Adolph set off, and after traveling for a time on the Eastern seaboard, he went to see the farming life of the Midwest.

In early 1849, Adolph wrote home to Frederika that although Americans were crude, compared to Europeans, they were also "tolerant, free, and independent." He added, "I already love our new country so much that I rejoice when I can sing its praises." America, he wrote, "is a triumph of the rights of man."

The three families had decided before Adolph left for the United States that they would live and work together on a large farm. For a time, Adolph hired himself out as a farmer in Ohio, but very soon he became convinced that farm life would not work out for the three families. He realized that the harsh conditions of farming in America would discourage them all.

For a while, he worked as a clerk in a grocery store in Cincinnati. Later, after all three families had arrived in America, he moved to Madison, Indiana, partly because he thought it was a growing town with great opportunities and partly to get away from the cholera that had taken the lives of many people in Cincinnati.

In September 1849, Adolph and Frederika were married in Madison, and during the next two years, Adolph operated a small starch factory as well as a small grocery and

The Brandeis family in 1855, a year before Louis's birth. *From left:* Amy, Frederika, Alfred, Adolph, and Fanny. UNIVERSITY OF LOUISVILLE ARCHIVES AND LIBRARY

produce store. Adolph's brother, Samuel, was a doctor, and when cholera attacked the citizens of Madison, he was very much in demand to help stem the dread disease. Frederika's brother, Lewis Dembitz, was a law student in Cincinnati, where he was very soon acclaimed as the brightest boy in his class by his teachers.

The hopes that the Brandeis family had had for Madison proved to be fruitless. People gradually began to move away to the bigger cities, and in 1851 the Brandeis couple, together with their first child, Fanny, moved to Louisville.

In 1852, Amy Brandeis was born, then Alfred, in 1854, and Louis on November 13, 1856. Adolph had set up a grain and produce business, and success was almost immediate. He formed a partnership with Charles Crawford in 1855, and soon the firm of Brandeis and Crawford operated a flour mill, a tobacco factory, an eleven-hundred-acre farm, and a river freighter that carried the name of the oldest Brandeis child, Fanny.

Soon Adolph's brother, Samuel, arrived in Louisville and built up a successful medical practice, while Lewis Dembitz, having passed the bar, opened a law office.

The Brandeises began to enjoy their life in Louisville. They built a large, comfortable home and staffed it with black servants. Young Louis, the baby of the family, played with his sisters' dolls, delighted in teasing little girls and scaring the maids in the house, and sometimes got into fistfights with the other boys in the neighborhood. Once he burned himself while playing with gunpowder. The family was close, and the two brothers, Alfred and Louis, enjoyed a special, warm relationship.

The Brandeis family had become relatively affluent and were now able to afford travel. Louis remembers visiting New York; Newport, Rhode Island; and Niagara Falls in Canada during the summer of 1864, when he was seven. When he was eighty-four years old, he still remembered that trip, especially the thrill of seeing "real Indians" for the first time.

Louis was not a Bar Mitzvah when he was thirteen. Although his parents did not hide their Jewish origins, they did not believe in the religious side of Judaism, nor did they actively involve themselves in the organized Jewish community. They always taught their children the importance of the ethical ideas of the Bible. Years later, Louis wrote that the "greatest combination of good fortune any man can have is a parentage unusual for both brains and character." Louis inherited from his father his good judgment, a sense of humor, and an ability to lead and inspire other people. From his mother he inherited a never-ending desire to improve the conditions of the world around him, a "sense of duty to the community—not so much by preaching but by practice."

Louis's mother wrote that "only goodness and truth and

## GERMAN AND ENGLISH ACADEMY.

### QUARTERLY REPORT

*Louis Brandeis*

From September 1st, to November 15th, 186

**EXPLANATION.**—The different grades of deportment and home study, and the progress in the various branches of instruction are indicated by the figures 6, 5, 4, 3, 2, 1. and 0; the figure 6 denoting perfection, the lower ones inferior grades. Studies without any mark are not taught in the class of the respective pupil.

Respectfully submitted to the Parents,

**W. N. HAILMAN,**
*Principal.*

Louis deserves special commendation for conduct and industry—

*W. N. Hailman*

One of Louis's grade-school report cards, commending him for his "conduct and industry" ZIONIST ARCHIVES AND LIBRARY

conduct that is humane and self-sacrificing toward those who need us can bring God nearer to us. Love, virtue, and truth are the foundation upon which the education of the child must be based. They endure forever."

Louis's uncle, Lewis Dembitz, was not only a lawyer but also an astronomer, a linguist, a mathematician, and a serious scholar of Jewish studies. He also became an observant Jew. Louis was one of his great admirers and decided, when he was still in his teens, to change his middle name from David to Dembitz, in honor of his mother's brother. Louis wrote that his uncle was "a living university—with him, life was an unending intellectual [adventure]." He would visit his uncle on the Sabbath and remember the "joy and awe with which my uncle welcomed the arrival of the day and the piety with which he observed it. I remember the extra delicacies, lighting of the candles, prayers over a cup of wine, quaint chants, and Uncle Lewis poring over books most of the day. I remember more particularly an elusive something about him which was spoken of as the 'Sabbath peace' and which years later brought to mind a passage from Addison in which he speaks of stealing a day out of life to live. Uncle Lewis used to say he was enjoying a foretaste of heaven."

In the Louisville high school, Louis dedicated himself to the study of French, Latin, German, chemistry, algebra, composition, and trigonometry—and seemed to master them all with ease. At the age of fifteen, he was graduated with honors. He read almost every kind of book he could get his hands on and worried about the direction his life would take. His father was a successful businessman, one uncle was a physician, and another a brilliant lawyer, but Louis himself was unsure what he wanted to do.

In 1872, a major recession descended on the United States. Louis's father decided to dissolve the family business, travel with his family to Europe for at least a year, and upon their return start afresh in a new venture. As things turned out, the Brandeis family remained in Europe for three years, and when they returned to America, Louis knew what he wanted to study—law.

Lincoln had been a lawyer, his beloved uncle was a lawyer, and Louis believed that becoming a lawyer would open up for him great areas of opportunity—for himself personally and for his deeply felt desire to be of service to the community.

# 2

# *Europe*

*Young men who feel drawn to the legal
profession may rest assured that they will
find in it an opportunity for usefulness
which is probably unequaled elsewhere.*

The Brandeis family sailed for Europe in the summer of 1872, planning to return toward the end of the following year. The parents and four children set out on what they were certain would be a fabulous journey of adventure. Louis, the youngest, was at fifteen already a lanky youth of six feet, possessing piercing blue eyes. Together with his parents, brother, and two sisters, he felt that life was good, and that the trip to visit Europe's cultural centers would be a high point of his life.

In his diary of August 10, 1872, written aboard the SS *Adriatic*, he wrote, "Our ship is a large ocean steamer, four thousand tons, four hundred feet in length, and said to be the fastest between England and America, having made one trip in seven days and eight hours. Our captain, a stout six-footer, is a jolly-looking man and makes himself as agreeable as possible."

The Brandeis family arrived first in Liverpool and then went on to London, where they visited the historic sites and museums before crossing the English Channel to the continent. Louis had been told that if he could pass the entrance exams of the Gymnasium, a kind of junior college in Vienna, he would be allowed to enroll and study there.

Although he had earned a gold medal when he was graduated from the Louisville high school, he did not succeed in passing the entrance examinations in Vienna. While the rest of the family traveled around Germany, Italy, and France sight-seeing, Louis remained in Vienna and studied privately and also took some courses at the university. He particularly liked expanding his knowledge of German and learning to appreciate the music that had helped make Vienna world famous.

In the spring of the following year, he rejoined his family in Italy, where his sister Amy had come down with typhoid fever. The Brandeis family remained in Milan until Amy recovered, and in the summer they all proceeded north to Switzerland.

Louis recalled the summer of 1873 with enthusiasm all his life. He and his brother joined their father in climbing the majestic Alps. Although he was strong and enjoyed the outdoors, Louis was not the athlete that his brother was, and he found it difficult to keep up with Alfred as they climbed ever higher into the Swiss mountains. It was a summer that both brothers would always remember.

Early in the fall, Louis made up his mind that he would like to study at the Annen-Realschule, a distinguished school in Dresden, Germany. He told his parents he wanted to make the trip alone and seek admission on his own. He was almost seventeen years old and had begun to feel the need to act independently.

When he arrived at the famous school, he had to steel himself before entering the principal's office. The school official said Louis would need to offer proof of birth and vaccination, to which he replied, "The fact that I'm here is proof of my birth, and you may look at my arm for evidence that I was vaccinated." There was something very special about the tall young man from America who spoke German with an American accent, and the principal decided to accept him without any formal tests.

He studied at the Dresden school for a year and a half, concentrating on languages, geography, physics, chemistry, mineralogy, mathematics, and literature. He found the courses and the teachers challenging and was awarded a prize for "industry and good behavior." Years later Louis said that the Dresden school taught him, most of all, how to think for himself.

The greatest lesson that Louis and his family learned from their extended European visit was how much they appreciated America. Louis recalled one incident when he came back to his dormitory in Dresden after hours. Having forgotten his key, he whistled to his roommate to toss down the key so that he could enter the building—an action for which he was strongly scolded. "In America," he used to explain, "you could whistle." He found that he could not accept the stern, almost military atmosphere of his classes and the formal respect that students were required to display to their teachers. The openness of America, the easy-going informality of the people, and the absence of strict distinctions between classes were rediscovered by Louis. He and his family returned to the United States in 1875, grateful for their travels throughout Europe and more fervent than ever in their attachment to America.

On the return voyage, Louis had time to reflect on his future. The idea of becoming a lawyer had begun to develop in his mind a few years earlier, and he decided that Harvard Law School, in Cambridge, Massachusetts, was where he wished to study. Before the summer, he applied for admission and was accepted. He then rejoined his family in Louisville, impatiently awaiting the opening of the semester in September, so that he could get on with his plans. He was not yet nineteen when he left his home in Kentucky for Cambridge and Harvard, not realizing at the time that he would spend the major part of his life first in the Boston area and later in Washington.

# 3

## Cambridge

*To think hard and persistently is painful.*

When Louis arrived at Harvard to begin his law studies, he was by no means a relaxed young man. His father had not been able to get his business going again, and Louis had been forced to borrow several hundred dollars from his older brother to see him through the first semester. His father and brother had opened a small retail store in Louisville and, from the letters that the two brothers exchanged almost every day, it was clear that the Brandeis family was not having an easy time back home.

Louis's father, who had always been an enthusiastic, hopeful kind of person, complained in a letter to his son that "misery loves company, and I have plenty of that now." Explaining that he spent much of his time trying to collect old debts, Adolph wrote to his young son at Harvard, "Enjoy this beautiful time with all your might and be conscious of it, because it won't always remain as beautiful as it is now, even if luck, with God's help, will favor you."

Louis's mother, Frederika Dembitz Brandeis ZIONIST ARCHIVES AND LIBRARY

Louis's mother shared his enthusiasm for life at Harvard. She wrote, "How pleasant your life in Cambridge is! How refreshing and wholesome this gay, intellectual atmosphere!" She assured him, however, that if things were not perfect, he could always turn to her. "I hope that you continue to write me about *yourself*—but everything, the disagreeable too, if it should come."

Louis was in love with life at Cambridge. He found the study of law just as challenging and rewarding as he had hoped it would be. He attended classes, took part in mock trials, joined a few social clubs, and sought out the company of the area's intellectual personalities of the day—people like Henry Adams and Ralph Waldo Emerson. He continued to read omnivorously and even found time to attend some lectures on art.

In a letter to his sister Amy, Louis wrote of the art lectures, "How wise one becomes—two weeks ago I should not have had any idea what all this means, and now I can write so learnedly on the subject!"

Years later, Louis remembered that he was filled with the "enthusiasm of youth" and entered into the spirit of Harvard with great hope and confidence for the future. The atmosphere of New England in general, and the Boston and Cambridge areas in particular, filled him with delight.

Sometimes he would stroll along the Charles River, and other times he would go rowing, a sport he enjoyed all his life. He remembered the influence of the early colonists of New England on the new nation's development. A son of immigrants who had fled to the safety and freedom of the United States, Louis felt a special sense of kinship with the early settlers and Founding Fathers of America. Although he was often lonesome for his family back in Louisville, he had already made up his mind that he wanted to live in New England. In that section of the country, the son of Bohemian Jews somehow felt that he had come home.

The Puritans who had settled Massachusetts had made a strong impression on the whole region. They believed that each person had a direct responsibility for shaping his life and making a success of his efforts. At the same time, they taught that everyone had to be aware of those in need and that service to the community was a very important part of people's lives. They believed that they were God's special people and even referred to themselves as the Chosen People, a term that is used in the Bible to describe the Jews. The Puritans were strongly moral, admired scholarship and hard work, and saw the great benefits of working together in congregations, schools, town halls, and institutions of higher learning. Through the Puritans' influence, the study of Hebrew became widely accepted at Harvard, for the Puritans admired the ideas of the Bible and the teachings of the Jewish people.

Louis immediately felt at home in this atmosphere, for he had been brought up by his family in a similar way—to strive for the best possible success, to serve the community, to be moral and upright, and to advance his knowledge and learning.

The leaders of the Boston and Cambridge communities who had been descended from the early Puritans came to be known as Brahmins. They were committed to each individual's struggle for success, and they taught the importance of being self-reliant and developing each person's abilities to the highest possible degree. These had been the same aims that Louis's family, especially his mother, had tried to instill in him and in his brother and sisters. Emerson, the famous writer from Boston, expressed these ideas in his work, and he became for Louis a lifelong source of inspiration.

In New England, respect for learning and study was the measure by which people were described. The famous author Mark Twain expressed it this way: "In Boston, they ask, how much does he know? In New York, how much is he worth? In Philadelphia, who were his parents?" Although Louis came from a Jewish family in Louisville, he swiftly earned the respect and admiration of his classmates and teachers because of his superb methods of study and his obvious talents as a future lawyer. As one of his friends expressed later, the fact that he was a Jew made him even more "remarkable—for he was a descendant of the great prophet Isaiah!"

While he was still in his teens, Louis had begun a system of self-education which took the form of copying down phrases and thoughts that he came across in his wide reading that he felt he wanted to refer to in the future. One such notation, found in his notebooks, was from Emerson. It reveals a great deal about the early development of Louis D. Brandeis. The notation from Emerson reads:

"Every man takes care that his neighbor shall not cheat

him. But a day comes when he begins to care that he does not cheat his neighbor. Then all goes well. He has changed his market cart into a chariot of the sun." This sense of responsibility for all people had been instilled in Louis by his family and was now made even stronger during his new life at Harvard.

When Louis arrived at Harvard, he was a poor Jewish youth from Kentucky, then regarded as a rather provincial area. All those around him recognized in his speech a Kentucky accent, which was in sharp contrast to the famous New England speech. Most of his fellow students came from wealthy families, and Harvard in that period had already become known as an intellectual and cultural stronghold of the United States. Louis also differed from other students in that he had been admitted to the law school without a college degree.

And yet when he left Harvard three years later, it was with the highest scholastic record ever attained at the law school. In fact, since he was still not yet twenty-two years old, a special ruling had to be taken by the school's board of trustees, allowing him to graduate under the age of the other students.

Louis supported himself at Harvard as a private tutor. He was very careful with his expenses, living on a minimum budget, and he even managed to save a few dollars during his student years. When he was able to repay his brother for having made it possible for him to enter law school, it gave him a sense of great achievement.

Various classmates saw at once that Louis was a very special kind of person. One classmate referred to his "keen intellectual face," while another said he had a "detectable Southern softness in his voice" and noted that he was a "black-haired, blue-eyed fellow, with high color suffusing his olive skin" who had the "polish and poise of a gifted actor."

Before he entered Harvard, Louis knew that most law-

yers in America learned their profession by reading law—
they would hire themselves out to lawyers and, acting as
clerks and apprentices, absorb as much legal knowledge as
they could before striking out on their own. Louis was for-
tunate that a new method of teaching law was begun just
before he became a law student. Known as the Langdell
method, it required students to attend special lectures on
various legal problems and then to be examined on those
problems. It was a more scientific way of teaching law than
had been used before and included analyzing specific cases
and learning from them. The new Harvard method gradually was adopted by most law schools throughout the country.

Louis described the new method as stating the case under study, examining the opinion of the court, reviewing
the arguments of the opposing lawyers, and criticizing the
reasoning upon which the court's decision was reached—
"the professor acting largely as moderator." Louis enjoyed
this case method and wrote later that it helped to create
"intellectual self-reliance and the spirit of investigation."

These were happy, exciting years for the young student;
he made careful notes of his lectures and the cases he studied. Many years later, when his daughter Susan began the
study of law, he sent her all of his notes and many of the
texts that he kept carefully arranged.

But Louis did not devote all of his time to classroom studies. He enjoyed making new friends among his fellow
students as well as among his professors. Gradually his
Harvard teachers and classmates began to introduce him to
some of the leaders of Boston during that period. He remembers hearing Emerson address a small group, and was
thrilled, he wrote to his sister, when he saw Longfellow at
a reception.

In one letter to his family, he wrote that although he was
happy and enjoying life at Harvard, "it must be confessed
that all Cambridge people are not necessarily intellectual

giants." He told of a party that he went to where some of the "young ladies who had the advantages of a European education concurred that Egypt is in Asia."

After attending a number of receptions and parties at which prominent people spoke or were honored, Louis began to realize that "very much of society would surely bore me." Slowly he developed a self-confident attitude in which he delighted in intelligence rather than in fame or society. His personal notebooks began to fill up with quotations from Shakespeare, Emerson, Tennyson, Matthew Arnold, Longfellow, and others. Early on, he began to practice what was later to become a typical Brandeis approach to life: He avoided idle chatter and searched continually for new and stimulating ideas.

When he was still living in Louisville, Louis had been taught to play the violin, but he had to admit that he was not very good at it. At law school he put away his violin for good, in a deliberate plan to create more time for his studies. He had written to his family that Harvard had a library of some fifteen thousand books, and he spent many long hours, it seemed, trying to read them all. The result could have been predicted—he developed serious eye strain and soon feared that he would lose his vision. (In those days, indoor reading was done by gaslight, which of course is inferior to modern electric lights.)

During the summer after his first year at Harvard, he consulted eye specialists in Cincinnati, Boston, and New York. All of them told him the same thing—he had to cut down on his reading or else he could lose his sight. When he returned to Harvard for his second year, he asked his friends to read to him, and that was how he completed his schooling. One unexpected advantage from this was that Louis developed an unusual memory, a gift that was to help him throughout his life.

In 1877 Louis was graduated from Harvard Law School cum laude. He decided, however, to remain in Cambridge for a year of graduate studies and was able to do so by continuing his tutoring and by proctoring exams at Harvard, for which he was paid a dollar an hour. (Costs at Harvard in those days were far, far less than they are today. A semester of study, which included use of the library, cost Louis $50.00, while board in the school's dining room came to $38.25 for the semester.)

Louis taught his private students, proctored exams, studied, and saved his money, continuing to live at the least possible expense. When he left Harvard in 1878, he had not only repaid his brother's loan but had managed to save more than $1,200, half of which he invested in bonds that paid an annual interest rate of 4 percent. Perhaps the knowledge that his father had had a difficult time earning money in his later years influenced Louis's approach to saving his extra funds and living modestly. This helped him, over a period of many years, to amass a fortune.

Now that his years of study were behind him, Louis suddenly found himself at a crossroads. He did not know which way to go. His family wanted him to return to Louisville, and his sister Fanny, who had married a lawyer and was living in St. Louis, urged him to come there and work in her husband's office. Louis's close friend from Harvard, Samuel Warren, proposed that they open a law office together in Boston. Another lawyer in St. Louis, James Taussig, wrote, offering him a job in his office. Louis himself seemed to want to remain at Cambridge, which he described in a letter to his family as "beautiful, and I am becoming more and more attached to the place."

Apparently he did not like the idea of working for his brother-in-law in St. Louis. The idea of forming a partnership with his friend and classmate Sam Warren must have troubled him mostly because he was afraid that Warren, who came from a prominent Boston family and had many excellent business contacts, would be the main source of business, and he would be put into an inferior position.

With some misgivings, Louis decided to accept the Taussig job offer in St. Louis. He was still a very young man and probably felt the need to be on his own rather than return home to Louisville. But he seems to have felt a little guilty about his decision, for he wrote to his mother in August 1878 that he "doubted somewhat whether I was right in the course I pursued in this matter. If you . . . think I was wrong, I most humbly beg your pardon." His mother replied immediately: "[You] had the right to follow your inclination, for you are so young you can afford a risk, and I am convinced that whatever you will undertake is going to be of advantage to you as a step in your development."

After spending the summer of 1878 tutoring the children of one of his law school professors and then recuperating from an illness, he left for St. Louis with obviously mixed feelings. Soon after his arrival, he began to feel he had made a mistake. He complained in a letter to his family about his salary, about the silly social life in the city, about the cases he was being given. He noted that the number of "young and old lawyers here without practice is appalling." He also came down with malaria, which further depressed and upset him. He had, in a very few years, become a New Englander, and he felt uncomfortable in St. Louis. His friend Warren continued to write him, urging that he return to Boston and that they set up an office together.

And then, out of the blue, Louis was informed by the chief justice of the Massachusetts Supreme Judicial Court that a job waited for him in Boston as secretary and assistant, which would pay $500 a year. The job, it turned out, had been arranged by three of Louis's former teachers at Harvard, who advised him that it would be "very valuable as a stepping stone." Most of the work, they wrote him, fell in the summer, and he would thus have time to devote to his own clients. Horace Gray, the chief justice, allowed Louis to be admitted to the bar of Massachusetts without having to wait for a formal examination.

Louis now notified his friend Sam Warren that he had decided to return to Boston and wished to establish a law partnership with him. He made it clear that he wanted to "become known as a practicing lawyer." He left St. Louis only eight months after having arrived there, happy to be returning to the Boston area and anxious to get on with his career. Soon after his arrival, the firm of Warren and Brandeis was established. The year was 1879, and Louis was still shy a few months of his twenty-third birthday.

# 4

## Boston

*I rise early because no day
is long enough for a day's work.*

Louis returned to Boston with a new enthusiasm for the city and the culture it represented. He felt lonesome for his family, but he worked hard in order to have no time for such sentiments. Each morning after breakfast he would take a long walk before entering the office of Justice Gray, where he spent his mornings. The salary he received for his work as a law clerk took care of all his needs for the next few years.

Following a spare lunch, he would go to his and his partner's office, where they worked together, trying to get the new law firm on the road to success. After dinner, he wrote his family, he would sometimes take care of his laundry, or go for an "evening sail" on a public boat, or visit the home of the Warren family. In Boston, he wrote, "one can enjoy living, and nature is so beautiful . . . heaven and earth, hills and water, nature and art."

Slowly, the two young partners began to develop a practice. Many of their early clients were friends from Harvard, and others were people active in public life. Gradually, through his clients, Louis became interested in Boston politics, social services, and the still-new labor movement. Louis's ability to remember a world of information helped him in many cases. One observer said that in the courtroom, he was quiet, gentle, one hand in his pocket—"but devastatingly thorough."

He found that he loved trial work, the challenge of new cases, and the wide variety of problems he had to solve. During this period, Harvard offered him a position as assistant professor of law, an offer he thought over very carefully before deciding against it. In his own mind, he knew what he wanted: to be financially independent and secure, and to attain a position where he would no longer have to work for money. The desire to be of service to the community continued to grow within him.

He remained extremely thrifty; living in simple rooms; eating plain, inexpensive food; and learning how to make the most of every hour of every day. His office was sparse. When he met with clients, he was direct and wasted no words. Some people thought he was cold, but he was determined not to waste precious time on meaningless conversations.

The experience of his eye strain had taught him a valuable lesson. He appreciated the importance of rest and relaxation and believed that nobody should work when tired. He often went horseback riding, canoeing, or sailing with his partner and with some new friends. One of these friends, a distinguished attorney himself, Oliver Wendell Holmes, Jr., invited Louis to spend weekends at his seashore home. Many years later, the two would sit together as justices on the bench of the United States Supreme Court, where Holmes was the chief justice.

During the 1880s, Louis worked very hard at enlarging his law practice. Little by little, his reputation as a trial lawyer grew, and more and more cases were brought to him. At the same time, he found himself taking an interest in the American labor movement, which was just beginning to develop. Although his own career was thriving, and he found himself working very hard, he never lost sight of the fact that on all sides there were great pockets of unemployment and poverty and social ills such as child labor that, to his mind, cried out for reform.

He was, in a real sense, a split personality: On the one hand, he was a highly successful corporation attorney earning very large fees, while on the other hand, his conscience and his sense of justice called out for him to help the needy. To a limited extent, he satisfied his yearning for doing good by taking on certain cases for a number of civic committees without fee.

By the time he was thirty-three, Louis had become one of the most prosperous and respected lawyers in all of New England. Sam Warren had left their law firm in 1889 to take over his family's business, and Brandeis now carried on alone, although he hired a number of young attorneys to assist him with his growing caseload. He and Warren remained friends for many years after their partnership was dissolved and together wrote an essay for lawyers titled "The Right to Privacy," which some people praised as a major contribution to America's interpretation of the law.

In 1890, tragedy struck. Louis's beloved sister Fanny, who had been mourning the untimely death of her young son, committed suicide. She died at the age of thirty-nine, and Louis was devastated by the news. He rushed home to Louisville to help comfort his parents. Together with his brother, Alfred, and his sister Amy, he tried to ease the pain of his parents. It was a difficult time for all the Brandeises.

During his visit to Louisville, Louis met a second cousin from New York whom he had last seen when she was six years old. Alice Goldmark was now twenty-four, slim, attractive, with large brown eyes and a soft, pleasing voice. She was a little shy in his presence, but he succeeded in getting her to talk freely and soon realized that they had many interests in common. He must have known that he had fallen in love and that she was to become his wife.

During the next few months, after he returned to Boston, Louis visited New York frequently to see Alice. In the summer of the same year, he spent several weeks at the Goldmark country home. Alice shared Louis's feelings and wrote in her diary about those months: "Louis's eyes are always upon me. We have found each other."

In March 1891, they were married in a private ceremony in New York by the bride's brother-in-law, Felix Adler, who had established the New York Society for Ethical Culture. Many members of the group had once been practicing Jews.

At that period of his life, Louis was almost totally divorced from Judaism and Jewish life. When he first learned that his sister Fanny had become ill, he wrote to his father that he believed in a Providence, and said that "man's work is so insignificant compared to that of the Creator." The God that Louis described was the Creator of all people, of all the world. The separateness of the Jews did not seem to interest him.

Clients came to Louis's office from all strata of society. One day the famous American author Mark Twain paid Louis a visit. He was interested in the possibility of suing someone for libel. Louis remembered the visitor very well later on—he was, to his amazement, dressed in shabby clothes and a long overcoat buttoned up to his neck. He never stopped pacing up and down the small office as he talked of the suit he was eager to press. Louis listened, weighed the evidence that the author presented, then advised him against going ahead.

Louis now carried a heavy burden. Not only was he in charge of the growing law firm, but because of his wife's frail health he found that he had to take care of many duties that fell under the heading of household chores. He paid the family bills, made all the arrangements for trips and house repairs, and did everything he could to free his wife of any unnecessary tasks. She shared with him the philosophy that he had developed—to live simply, to save, and to be able to serve the community.

Two daughters were born to the Brandeis couple: Susan, in 1893, and Elizabeth, three years later. Louis doted on his children and especially delighted in having an early breakfast with them, discussing their schoolwork, and as they grew older, the events of the day. He continued to follow his strong beliefs about rest and relaxation, and whenever possible he would leave his office at five in the afternoon and go horseback riding or canoeing on the Charles River before heading home for dinner.

He made it a practice also of taking off August of every year, having learned that "I could do twelve months' work in eleven months, but not in twelve." One August, he and a group of friends toured "the wilderness of Canada, fleeing from overcivilized Boston for the forest." Another summer he spent the whole month fishing, walking, canoeing, and climbing mountains, also in eastern Canada.

As his law firm grew, Louis added new lawyers to the staff. In 1897, the firm's name was changed to Brandeis, Nutter and Dunbar—two of his former employees having been named partners. The still relatively young lawyer—in 1897 he was only forty-one years old—was prospering. As he became more and more wealthy, Louis began to give some of his money to needy relatives and, later, to friends.

It was around this time that he began to sense that something had changed for him in Boston. There had developed in the city a new kind of closed political organization, thanks to the influx of Irish immigrants. Largely Catholic, the newcomers did not seem to him to have the same kind of ideals that Louis had found so attractive in the early years of

Louis in 1894, at thirty-eight  ZIONIST ARCHIVES AND LI-
BRARY

Massachusetts. Politics acquired religious and racial over-
tones, and Louis found himself feeling like an outsider.

He had always had a strong inclination to help the un-
derdog, and he did not feel comfortable with the German
Jewish community in Boston, most of whose members were
conservative and anti-liberal. As a Jew, although only a

nominal one, he was not accepted by the Jewish leadership of Boston. At the same time, the eastern European Jews, many of whose leaders and members did share Louis's progressive ideas, seemed to him distant relatives with whom he had little in common.

Although he did not belong to a synagogue, he made modest contributions to local Jewish charities. He had gradually become a very wealthy man from his law practice, but his charitable contributions did not reflect that. He took pride in the fact that Felix Adler, a great moral leader, was related to him through his wife, but he was at the same time aware of the fact that his own brother, Alfred, had married a Christian and seemed to be happy. The problems of the Jewish people did not touch him.

It is difficult to understand Louis during this period of his life. His beloved uncle Lewis Dembitz had begun to emerge in the American Jewish community as a leading Jewish scholar, an early follower of all causes designed to aid persecuted Jews overseas, and as a leading political figure in Kentucky. Dembitz never wavered in his religious observance, a fact that Louis perhaps tried but did not ever succeed in understanding.

During this same time span, the situation of the Jewish people in Europe had continued to worsen. In Russia, where the vast majority of the world's Jews lived at the time, and which was under the cruel domination of the Czarist government, pogroms (organized attacks) against defenseless Jews had broken out in the 1880s. As early as 1879, an openly anti-Semitic movement had sprung up in Germany. Every trouble that existed in that country was held to be the fault of the Jews, who were described as inferior to their fellow Aryan citizens. The Jews in Germany were blamed for being too prominent in the world of business as well as in the arts and sciences. More than a quarter-million Germans signed a petition to the German chancellor demanding an immediate end to all Jewish immigration to the country. Jews who had not been baptized were unable to teach at a university, get a job in a government office, or hold a commission in the armed forces.

The anti-Semitic movement expanded to the east and west. French bankers tried to convince the public to invest their funds only in banks sponsored by the French Catholic community. In 1882, in Dresden, where Louis had studied for a year and a half when he was a teenager, an officially proclaimed international anti-Semitic congress was held.

In April 1881, large outbreaks of barbaric attacks against small Jewish communities took place across Russia. Many people were killed; many women were raped; hundreds of homes, synagogues, and stores were destroyed. The violence and hatred spread to Warsaw, Poland. Soon there were thousands upon thousands of Jews fleeing the savagery of Russia and Poland to the relative freedom of the Western world. Protest demonstrations were held in London and Paris. The American minister in Russia registered a protest to the Czarist officials, and a similar protest was heard in the House of Commons in the British capital.

The cruelties inflicted against the Russian Jews continued into the 1890s. Similar pogroms broke out in Romania. Violent attacks against Jews took place in Kishinev in 1903 and continued for a period of several more years. The massacres were estimated to have taken place in nearly three hundred communities, resulting in the death of more than fifty thousand Jews.

In 1894, a French army captain, Alfred Dreyfus, was accused of having given military secrets to the Germans. The charges were later proven to be totally false and had been the result of a conspiracy of French anti-Semites. The Dreyfus trial in Paris became a world event. Thousands of Frenchmen and most of the press demanded that he be executed. The next year, Dreyfus was sent to Devil's Island to serve a life sentence, having protested throughout the trial that he was innocent.

Four years later, in 1899, Dreyfus was brought back to France and cleared of all charges. As a result of the clearly trumped-up trial, a young Jewish correspondent from Austria (he was born in Budapest, then part of the Austro-Hungarian Empire) by the name of Theodor Herzl came to the conclusion that the only way that Jews in danger would be able to survive would be to have a country of their own.

He sat down and wrote a small book, *The Jewish State.* In 1897, in Basel, Switzerland, the first World Zionist Congress was held, in which delegates from almost every part of the world gathered and vowed to establish a Jewish homeland where Jews would no longer be persecuted.

There was, during this period of the 1880s, 1890s, and early 1900s, a vast refugee immigration to the United States and to England of thousands of Jews. Decent people of all groups had bitterly denounced the pogroms in eastern Europe and the false charges brought in France against Dreyfus. And in many parts of the world, thousands of Jews had been deeply stirred by the call of Herzl and the early Zionist leaders for a Jewish homeland.

And yet despite all this turmoil, Louis Brandeis was, so far as is known, uninvolved. If he cared about his fellow Jews across the sea, he did not voice his sentiments in public. As a lawyer of distinction, his voice would certainly have been listened to, if he had spoken out against the French for their rigged trial of Dreyfus. With one exception, he remained publicly silent throughout this period.

The exception was the emergence of Herzl and his Zionist idea. Louis reacted to the idea of a return of the Jews to their ancient homeland favorably. He said that this was a movement that he could become involved in. He liked it.

Ironically, many years later, when the name of Louis Brandeis came up as a possible member of the cabinet that the new president, Woodrow Wilson, was forming, Brandeis defended himself by citing those who criticized him as using the same tactics that were used in the trial of Dreyfus.

# 5

## A Need for Change

*Struggle is the law of life. Must we
not fight, all of us, even for the peace
that we most crave?*

In the Boston of the late nineteenth century, Louis had not
come up against any great displays of anti-Semitism. He
himself had been accepted by the most exclusive clubs. Although his daughters were enrolled in prestigious Boston
schools and occasionally reported that their teachers liked
to single out those students who came from the "old families," he did not consider this to be a serious problem.

What really troubled him in this period of his life was the
growing chasm between the rich and the poor. Having himself succeeded in becoming a very rich man, he felt that
every young American should have an opportunity to climb
up the economic ladder. He realized, however, that economic conditions in America were changing rapidly and
making the change from poor to rich was becoming harder.
He believed that the dramatic rise of industry and the de-
cline of farming were major reasons for the new situation,

and felt strongly that these were not reasons to lock people up in an economic prison.

He once wrote, "Half a century ago, nearly every American boy could look forward to becoming independent as a farmer or mechanic, in business or professional life; and nearly every American girl might expect to become the wife of such a man. Today most American boys have reason to believe that throughout life they will work in some capacity as employees of others, either in private or public business; and a large number of women occupy like positions."

In short, he believed that big business in America had become too big, and that for the great majority of people this development meant a second-rate life.

While still in his thirties, Louis was greatly successful by any standards. Whereas most lawyers at that time were earning $5,000 a year, he was earning $50,000. By 1907, he had succeeded in building his fortune to $1 million, and before he became a member of the Supreme Court, he had added another million from his investments. When he died, he left an estate of $3 million, the major part of which he left to charity—after having throughout his lifetime given away an additional $1.5 million.

He had come to realize that to a very large degree the courts and the law itself in America had not kept up with changing conditions in America. He said that "out of the facts grows the law," by which he meant that laws should be based on real-life situations rather than on old laws that might have been suitable many years earlier.

He was not alone in his feelings. His old friend, Oliver Wendell Holmes, Jr., who became a member of the Supreme Court in 1902, also urged the need for reform in many areas of daily life. Louis began to speak out on the existing problems that faced the country, which he summarized as simply the law of the land not having kept up with the needs of the day.

In one speech, Louis declared that while political, social,

and economic sciences had noted the changing needs and times, the field of law had remained "largely deaf and blind to them." He complained that the "courts continued to ignore newly arisen social needs." He criticized the law for having a "tendency to lag behind the facts of life."

Louis looked upon his work as a means for representing not only his client but, more importantly, for representing the best interests of the largest number of people involved. He offered advice to businessmen that would help them and at the same time would benefit the greatest possible number of people.

In one case, a manufacturer of shoes asked for his help in a labor problem. He wanted his workers to take a large cut in pay because times were bad, and his employees had previously been well paid. Louis questioned his client for some time and discovered that many of the workers had been laid off during the year in slow periods. He proposed that his client reorganize his business to space out the production of shoes throughout the year rather than during a few peak months. The advice was accepted, and it turned out to be helpful not only to the workers, who now had jobs all year long, but also to the company's stockholders.

Gradually, Louis began to devote more and more of his time and energies to public service. He also called on his fellow lawyers to do the same thing, claiming that "able lawyers have allowed themselves to become adjuncts of great corporations and have neglected their obligation to use their powers for the protection of the people. We hear much of the 'corporation lawyer' and far too little of the 'people's lawyer.' The great opportunity of the American bar is and will be to stand again as it did in the past, ready to protect also the interests of the people."

With time, Louis began to be known first in Boston and then in all parts of the country as the people's attorney. He refused to accept any fees for his public service and once told a close friend that he had already determined to devote one full hour every day to public causes, and planned to expand that to half of his working day. In fact, after a time, as he devoted increasing hours of the day to various public needs, he began to feel that he was being unfair to his partners in the law firm that bore their names. He started to pay the law firm for the time he was taking away from his office, a step that was so unusual that he was questioned by the Boston press about it.

People in general and the reporters in Boston in particular kept trying to understand him; many undoubtedly were looking for hidden motives. They wanted to know why he was giving so much free time to various public causes, and why he did not instead simply make large donations to worthy causes. His reply at one occasion speaks for itself.

"Some men buy diamonds and rare works of art. Others delight in automobiles and yachts. My luxury is to invest my surplus effort, beyond that required for the proper support of my family, to the pleasure of taking up a problem and solving, or helping to solve, it for the people, without receiving any compensation. Your yachtsman or automobilist would lose much of his enjoyment if he were obliged to do for pay what he is doing for the love of the thing itself. So I should lose much of my satisfaction if I were paid in connection with public service of this kind. I have only one life, and it is short enough. Why waste it on things I don't want most? I don't want money or property most. I want to be free."

At another time, Louis expressed his beliefs in a brief phrase: "The greatest happiness in life is not to donate but to serve."

One of the traits that distinguished Louis Brandeis from many other lawyers was his strong feeling that, before he undertook a case, whether professionally or as a service to the community, he had to be certain that the side he represented was morally correct.

He also strongly believed that lawyers had a duty to educate both themselves and the public at large on everything in life that could affect the law. He urged his fellow lawyers that instead of talking about a contract's fine points, they should teach judges and the public the true situation that existed in an industrialized America.

The latter years of the nineteenth century were a time of great industrial ferment in America. Between 1860 and 1900, some 676,000 patents for new inventions were granted. The telephone came into wide use; a transatlantic cable was laid in 1866; copper mines were opened in Montana; oil fields were developed in Texas, Oklahoma, Illinois, and other states; and coal mining was expanded in Pennsylvania and West Virginia.

Thomas Jefferson had conceived of the United States emerging as one of the great agricultural nations of the world, but Brandeis quickly came to realize that America was changing very rapidly and was being transformed into an industrialized giant. He continued to show deep concern that this rapid economic change in America would be carried out at the expense of millions of ordinary Americans, who, he feared, would be exploited by huge corporations. Although he must surely have known that progress could not be halted, Louis became more determined than ever to help the working population of America from being overworked, underpaid, and employed in hazardous surroundings.

# 6

## People's Attorney

*Justice can be attained only by a*
*careful regard for fundamental facts,*
*since justice is but truth in action.*

Now a highly successful lawyer, Louis began to move in a new direction in his work. Filled with anger at what he felt were abuses against large numbers of people who did not have well-paid lawyers to defend their rights, he took on cases that would improve the working and living conditions for huge numbers of people.

It was not long before his fame as a people's attorney spread to all parts of the United States. He continued to press for those ideals he believed in deeply. Many years later, when he was appointed to the Supreme Court, he did not change his views and, because some of his opinions were at times unpopular, he came to be known as the great dissenter.

Although he was essentially a careful, conservative man, his critics labeled him a radical, a charge he usually just ignored. In fact, he believed in the American capitalist system—but he wanted to regulate it so that no abuses would be allowed that would surely injure the well-being of thousands of people.

He joined a wide variety of reform groups and did not hesitate to attack the most well-entrenched interests in the nation. When superwealthy railroad barons tried to establish a monopoly over the railroad system of New England, he battled them successfully for a period of six years, from 1909 to 1914.

A lover of the outdoors, he campaigned against certain interests that he felt were abusing the country's land resources. Conservation, to Louis, meant protecting the forests and the rivers and the vast areas of America for future generations.

In all his legal battles, both as the people's attorney and later when he was a Supreme Court justice, he tried to show that every law had to be interpreted in light of the changing needs of the day. He maintained his view that big corporations had to be carefully watched; otherwise, he explained, they had a strong tendency to exploit their bigness at the expense of the people. He went even further and warned that unless big business was regulated by law, there was a danger that America's democracy would be diminished.

In the early part of the twentieth century, he became an adviser to Woodrow Wilson, who later became president of the United States. The ideas he proposed to Wilson eventually became basic laws of the United States. The Federal Reserve Act (limiting the power of banks), the Clayton Antitrust Act (preventing monopolistic business), and the Federal Trade Commission Act (regulating commerce across the nation) all had their origins in programs first outlined by Brandeis.

American industry in the late nineteenth century and the early part of the twentieth century expanded dramatically. The gross national product (GNP) of the United States continued to get bigger and bigger, particularly in the industrial and manufacturing areas. It was during this expansion period that millions of immigrants arrived in the United States. They were warmly welcomed because huge numbers of people were needed to work in the mines, the mills, and the factories.

Many of these immigrant workers lived in hovels, crowded ten or twelve people to a room, often without the basic necessities. Children, some of them no more than seven or eight years old, were put to work for long hours in textile mills. In the dark and often dangerous coal mines, young boys of ten or twelve worked alongside the adult miners. It was not unusual for them to work twelve hours a day, seven days a week. Cave-ins, explosions, and coal dust helped in many cases put an end to their wretched lives.

In the large cities, garment workers labored under the most difficult conditions, many of them eventually dying from tuberculosis. In 1911, in New York, there was a horrible fire in a factory that had not installed proper safety devices. One hundred and forty-six young women died in the inferno.

Louis saw all these and other events taking place around him, and his determination to institute reforms grew stronger. He knew that there were some millionaires who spent more money on one party than a young factory worker could hope to earn in a whole lifetime—and he was convinced that such a sharp contrast in earning power could lead to the end of American freedom and democracy.

He battled against a Boston company that tried to monopolize the public transportation system, believing that this would harm the public at large. He saw in the companies that provided gas for lighting in Boston an opportunity for a public utility, and helped to develop this concept. He continued to maintain his view that stockholders of a company were entitled to a fair return on their investment, but not at the cost of the public as a whole.

He learned that poor workers, anxious to protect their families in case of the family breadwinner's death, were paying twice as much for insurance protection as their employers. He made an intensive study of life-insurance practices and finally came up with the idea of low-cost insurance that would be sold by savings banks—a step that would protect poor people and at a price that was affordable. The big insurance companies attacked him for what they described as leading the nation down the road to socialism. Many savings bank directors at first did not understand the long-range importance of Louis's plan, and they too joined in the assaults on him.

By now, Brandeis had learned a painful lesson: It was important to win over public support for a new program. He began to do something that he had never done before— he launched a series of talks to explain his proposal to business, labor, civic, and other organizations. Sometimes he spoke twice in one evening at different gatherings. Gradually he also learned the importance of getting the press to report on his talks so that ever more people would begin to understand what it was he was trying to achieve.

Brandeis, in his savings-bank life-insurance program, was totally convinced of the justice and fairness of his idea. He continued for years to try to obtain support from the banks themselves, and later he also had to win the approval of the state governments. Many people, of course, thought he was a visionary, a dreamer. One publication in the insurance field mocked him, claiming that "nobody need lose any sleep over the dream of the Boston theorist, for the dream has about one chance in a million of ever coming true." But in 1908 the plan went into effect in Massachusetts. And today savings-bank life insurance is an established fact of life in America, providing protection for millions at low cost.

Louis never seemed to falter in his self-appointed mission. He worked to establish minimum wages for employees and for laws that would limit the number of hours that women were required to work each day. He gradually began to take a serious interest in the labor union movement, and soon decided that the country's workers deserved to have unions to represent their interests.

Nevertheless, he warned, "If unions are lawless, restrain and punish their lawlessness; if their demands are unreasonable or unjust, resist them; but do not oppose unions as such." He soon became convinced that one of the main problems of many unions and their members was the uncertainty of their jobs. Many workers had accepted the situation of high employment during certain seasons and equally high unemployment during other times—a condition that Brandeis felt would always lead to unrest.

He was shocked when the Supreme Court, in 1905, threw out a New York State law that had allowed bakers to work no more than ten hours per day. Hard as it is to believe nowadays, the highest court in the nation had ruled that such a law was "meddlesome interference with the rights of the individuals."

A few years later, Brandeis argued before the Supreme Court for a minimum-wage law in Oregon, which he hoped would eventually be adopted by all the states of the union. One of the judges commented on Louis's appearance that "here stood a man who knew infinitely more, and who cared infinitely more, for the vital daily rights of the people than the men who sat there sworn to protect them."

In his arguments for minimum wages, Brandeis ignored previous legal decisions. Instead, he talked of the effects of overwork on the health of the women workers and listed medical data from all parts of the world supporting his thesis. He continued to hammer home to the Supreme Court the need to recognize the terrible situation in a highly industrialized America.

The words and the photograph of Louis D. Brandeis were now being studied all over the United States. As he grew older, some people said, he began to look more and more like his boyhood idol, Abraham Lincoln. And like Lincoln, he was ready to fight for an America that would be "of the people, by the people, [and] for the people."

His reputation as a friend of labor who could also see the other side of a labor dispute had traveled far and wide. Tens of thousands of garment workers in New York, most of them Jewish immigrants from eastern Europe, were suffering from a long strike. The union leaders insisted on having a closed shop—where only union members could be employed—while their employers refused even to consider such an idea. The strike to some people looked as though it might go on forever, affecting the multimillion-dollar garment industry and leaving many thousands of families without any income or hope.

Both sides agreed to ask Brandeis to come to New York to help settle the strike. The year was 1910, and as a result of the strike and his work to end it so that both sides would be satisfied, Brandeis's life from that point on took an entirely new direction.

In New York, among the eastern European Jews with whom he had had almost no contact in the past, Brandeis rediscovered his Jewishness.

# 7

## A Zionist

*We have survived persecution
because of the virtues and
sacrifices of our ancestors.*

The summer of 1910 was hot and humid. The tempers of the twenty people—ten from the union and ten from the employers—who met in a conference room to see if Brandeis could mediate the dispute between them were frayed. Nearly seventy thousand people were involved, directly and indirectly in the strike, and the owners of the garment factories in New York were losing money every day that the strike continued.

There was, of course, in those days no air-conditioning. Brandeis had given up a planned vacation to try to help cool things down and end the strike so that both sides would be able to work together in the future. Sitting at the head of the long conference table, he was the only man in the room who continued to wear a jacket. All the other people in the room looked hot, angry, impatient, and skeptical about the man with the blue eyes who spoke differently from them, who had the trace of a southern accent, and who seemed so calm.

Speaking softly but firmly, he explained that he wished to help end the strike for the good of the workers, the factory owners, and the public. What is more, he continued, he also wanted to find a formula that would prevent any future strikes in the garment industry. He talked of fairness and justice for the workers, and quickly won them over to him. It took a little longer for Louis to gain the confidence of the employers, but he won their trust too.

After a time, he came up with a proposal that he felt would be fair to both sides and that would bring peace to the industry. Instead of a rigid closed shop, he suggested a preferential union shop, an entirely new idea, which would give preference in hiring to union members. For a while, both sides resisted his proposal, and then in a relatively short time, he got them to agree. The long strike was over, both sides seemed satisfied, and Brandeis was acclaimed as a hero for his work. He was named a permanent arbitrator to help iron out any possible future disputes.

Brandeis was happy to leave the humid New York atmosphere for his summer home on Cape Cod. He was pleased that he had been able to help settle the dispute, and he had time now to think over the strange feelings he had had when he was working with the immigrant Jews in New York.

He realized that he had never before really known Jews from Russia and Poland—people whose principal language was Yiddish—who had been steeped in biblical and Talmudic teachings, some of whom were avid socialists and others who were deeply observant Jews, very much like his beloved uncle, Lewis Dembitz.

It has been a strange, unsettling experience for him. He had become accustomed to the spirit of New England and had been brought up in a home that was only nominally Jewish. These Yiddish-speaking immigrants, he thought, were different from the German Jews he had known in Boston, Louisville, and St. Louis. They had a certain enthusiasm and spirit that he admired. During the long hours in the conference room where the issues of the strike were raised and fought over, he recalled, one of them had quoted from the prophet Isaiah. He remembered the lines:

"The Lord will enter into judgment with the elders of His people, and the princes thereof: 'It is you that have eaten up the vineyard, the spoil of the poor is in your houses. What do you mean by crushing My people, and grinding the face of the poor?' "

The worker had cited prophetic verses to complain against being exploited by the bosses. One of the workers had thundered, "We sweat for a living—they expect us to be thankful for a few crumbs. We labor long hours under inhuman conditions while they make fortunes!"

Brandeis now believed that the Jewish workers he had come to know in New York, the so-called masses from eastern Europe and Russia who had fled the pogroms and the oppression of the Czarist regime, and who were laboring long hours to establish themselves in America, had more of the idealism and spirit of justice than the people he lived among in New England. Indeed, he saw them as being very similar in many ways to the Puritans and the Founding Fathers of America.

He began to think about his life, his family, his roots. He had never identified actively with the Jewish community, although he continued to contribute small sums to Boston Jewish charities. He had gone to battle for the oppressed of America, but he had never done anything special to help the refugees of his own people from Europe, nor had he spoken out forcefully at the time of the notorious Dreyfus trial in France.

He realized that, although he had never tried to disguise his origins, he had remained aloof from the Jewish community. Even though he was by now a national figure, the *Jewish Encyclopedia*, published in 1905, did not even mention him. He had, he recalled, once expressed himself favorably about Herzl and the new Zionist movement, but he had done nothing concrete to show his support or interest.

After his experience with the garment workers in New York, he wrote that he had found a sense of ethics on both sides of the strike that he had never come across before. "What struck me most," he said, "was that each side had a great capacity for placing themselves in the other fellows' shoes. There was the usual bitterness, but despite this, each side was willing to admit the reality of the other fellows' predicament. They really understood each other and admitted the understanding. They argued but were willing to listen to argument. That set these people apart in my experience in labor disputes."

There is a tradition among Jews that there exists in every Jewish person what is called in Yiddish a *pintele Yid*, or "a tiny spark of Jewish identity." It means that no matter how distant one may be from Jewish life and from the Jewish community, somehow, somewhere, there remains in that person an eternal link to the Jewish people.

Brandeis, it seemed, had found that he too, at the age of fifty-four, had a *pintele Yid* inside his tall, lanky person.

In the fall of that same year, the editor of a Jewish newspaper in Boston, Jacob de Haas, came to visit Brandeis. He was looking for some legal advice in connection with his paper, the *Jewish Advocate*. He was a personable man and spoke with a British accent. He mentioned in passing that he had been the secretary of Theodor Herzl, who had died six years earlier at the age of forty-four.

Brandeis was intrigued by the newcomer. He asked him what the most important issue of the day was among the Jewish people, freely admitting that he knew very little about such things. De Haas replied at once that the single most critical problem of the Jews was Zionism, the program to restore the Jewish people to their ancient homeland and to put an end, once and for all, to nearly two thousand years of Jewish suffering.

There seemed to be an electric, even mystical moment in the air as the two men sat in Brandeis's study regarding each other. Explaining that his wife was away, Brandeis invited his guest to stay for lunch and tell him more about the new Zionist movement. De Haas gladly accepted. Throughout lunch and for several hours into the afternoon, Brandeis listened attentively as his guest talked about the Zionist movement, its origins and its goals, about Herzl, and about the dangerous situation for Jews in many European and in some Asian and North African countries. Brandeis's daughters—Elizabeth, who was now fourteen, and Susan, seventeen—sat wide-eyed while de Haas spoke and their father questioned him about the early Jewish pioneers—known as *halutzim*—who had already started the first new settlements in Palestine, which was then part of the Ottoman (Turkish) Empire.

The unplanned hours-long meeting between Brandeis and de Haas turned out to be a momentous occasion. Suddenly, Brandeis was able to see that the Zionist program was something that he could support with his whole heart. It was the kind of challenge that Brandeis enjoyed, and the end goal was an ideal to which he could relate. Brandeis understood immediately that one did not have to be religious, which he was not, to support the new movement. Here, as Brandeis saw it, was an historic opportunity to correct a wrong against a whole people, a wrong that had existed for nearly two thousand years.

That evening Brandeis wrote to his brother in Louisville, "I had by chance one of the original Zionists for lunch. . . . I am going to become a Zionist."

He began by reading Jewish history and many books dealing with Jewish issues. In 1911 and 1912, he continued to learn everything he could about the new movement and about the Jewish people, past and present. But there was so little time! He remained constantly occupied with his wide-ranging campaigns as the people's attorney. He was also meeting more and more frequently with Woodrow Wilson, who won the election in 1912 for the presidency of the United States, outlining his ideas on future new laws that would help America's economy and at the same time protect the rights of all its people.

Wilson was elected in November and was to be inaugurated the following March, as was the practice in those days. Rumors began to circulate that the president-elect planned to nominate Brandeis as attorney general of the United States. These rumors were almost immediately met with loud protests from Brandeis's enemies, who said he was an unreliable radical.

There continued an anti-Brandeis barrage on the White House, as Wilson took on his duties, that must surely have been disturbing to Brandeis, but he generally ignored the reports. He believed in achievement, in attaining positive results, not in trading insults. President Wilson did not name him to any government positions but continued to consult him frequently on many issues.

How he managed to juggle all his interests and commitments is hard to imagine. He had joined the Federation of American Zionists and began to speak on their behalf in various parts of the country. Brandeis's participation in the Zionist movement was a great plus, for he was known throughout the United States not only as the people's attorney but as an adviser to the president. He visited Wilson and many of his colleagues in the new Democratic administration frequently. And he continued to read and study reports on every aspect of Zionist interest.

When someone once asked him how he could manage to do so much, he replied that with self-discipline every person could double and even triple his efficiency and productivity. He was an early riser, up and at work by 5:30 A.M., although he tried to go to bed at 10. He was also, he explained, never a worrier. He said he was a citizen who had a deep sense of the American ideals of life, liberty, and the pursuit of happiness. He explained, "Life, in this sense, means living, not existing; liberty, freedom in things industrial as well as political; happiness includes among other things that satisfaction that can come only through the full utilization and development of one's faculties."

For Brandeis, the ideals of Zionism, as he saw them, envisaged a small state where the perennially endangered Jews would be able to live without fear of persecution. The concept of a small Jewish homeland that would stress the quality of life over material goals excited him. He saw Zionism as an extension of the ideals of the early Puritans, with its emphasis on self-reliance, hard work, and equality for all.

By 1913, in the same year that Wilson was inaugurated president, Brandeis had been elected associate executive committeeman of the Zionist federation. The next year he was elected to represent American Zionists at the World Zionist Congress, but he declined on the ground of not having the time to spare from his other duties. He did, however, send a message to the congress, held in Vienna, urging that they concentrate their efforts in three areas: Jews who were immigrating to other countries should be encouraged to head for Palestine; negotiations with the Turkish government, which ruled Palestine, should be started in order to obtain large concessions of land; and a worldwide effort should be launched to provide capital and know-how to set up suitable industrial plants in Palestine.

Not everyone in the United States in that period was in agreement with Brandeis's new role as a Zionist leader. The bulk of the Reform Jews, led by Cincinnati's Rabbi Isaac M. Wise, insisted that the whole Zionist program was wrong. America, they proclaimed, is the "new Zion." Most of these Reform Jews were of German origin and privately voiced a fear that if they backed a Jewish homeland in Palestine, they would be accused by their fellow Americans of double loyalty, a viewpoint that Brandeis found ridiculous.

In fact, Brandeis spoke out openly on this issue, declaring, "Let no man imagine that Zionism is inconsistent with patriotism. Multiple loyalties are objectionable if they are inconsistent. A man is a better citizen of the United States for being also a loyal citizen of his state, and of his city; for being loyal to his family, and to his profession or trade; for being loyal to his college or his lodge. Every Irish-American who contributed towards advancing home rule was a better man and a better American for the sacrifice he made. Every American Jew who aids in advancing the Jewish settlement in Palestine, though he feels that neither he nor his descendants will ever live there, will likewise be a better man and a better American for doing so."

Brandeis spent the summer of 1914 reading heavily on Jewish issues. When war broke out in Europe in August, he understood that a major new crisis had been thrust upon the whole world, and that very special actions would have to be taken to protect the tiny gains that the Zionist movement had achieved in Palestine.

# 8

## War Years

*The suffering of the Jews due to injustices*
*continuing throughout nearly twenty centuries*
*is the greatest tragedy in history.*

When World War I broke out in Europe, it seemed at times that nobody really wanted to wage war. On the other hand, no one seemed to know how to prevent it. Germany, the Austrian-Hungarian empire, and Turkey were united on one side against France, England, Russia, and many smaller European nations. The United States remained neutral until 1917, when she entered the war on the Allied side against the Germans.

For the Jewish communities of Russia, long oppressed by the hated Czarist regime, the war was a disaster. All that seemed to lie ahead for them was more bloodshed and death. German Jews found themselves fighting French and British Jews, and no doubt many of them felt unhappy about the strange turn that history had taken.

The small Jewish community in Palestine, unhappy under the cruel regime of the Turks, did not feel strong enough to resist their rulers, although there is little doubt that the overwhelming majority of the Jewish population rooted for an Allied victory. Independence at that time seemed far off in the distance, and the Jews would have preferred to be under British or French rule rather than under the oppressive Turks.

For the Zionists, the war posed a difficult problem. The headquarters of the world Zionist movement had been in Berlin, and now that Germany had gone to war against Russia, Britain, and France, with their large Jewish populations, it was essential that Zionist headquarters be moved immediately to a neutral place. The only possible choice was the United States, even though the movement in America had continued to remain relatively small and weak.

An emergency meeting was called for August 30, 1914, in New York, to review the critical situation that the Zionist movement now found itself in, and to obtain immediate funds for the small Palestinian Jewish community, whose well-being was especially worrisome since Germany was allied with Turkey.

Brandeis was among those who was asked to come to the meeting. Many of the early American Zionist leaders had mixed feelings about him. It was true that he was a confidant of the president of the United States and was a respected national figure. It was also true that he had joined the Zionist federation two years earlier and had gone out to speak on its behalf. But he had never before done anything of substance for the group, and his seemingly thin link to the Jewish people put some of the leaders off. Nevertheless, the people attending the meeting realized that they would have to name someone of stature to head the new emergency committee that was being formed by the various Zionist groups in the United States. And it would be helpful if that person could help donate and raise the large sums of money needed in the period ahead.

The conference named Brandeis to serve as head of the

Provisional Executive Committee for General Zionist Affairs. To the surprise of some of the delegates, he accepted. He spoke about the serious conditions that existed for Jews in the areas of Europe already suffering in the war zones. He cited facts and figures, which amazed many of those in attendance who had assumed that he would simply be a good figurehead. He announced the immediate launching of an emergency fund and announced his own $1,000 gift, which was soon followed by other large donations.

The delegates attending the emergency meeting were pleased with themselves, and many of them began to leave for home. None of them had any idea what kind of man Brandeis was. As chairman, he asked the leaders of the various groups within the committee to stay on so that he could learn a little more from them about some of the specific problems that each group in the Zionist movement had, and how they were planning to solve the problems.

The delegates agreed. After all, Brandeis was a famous American Jew and President Wilson's adviser, so an extra hour or two to discuss some of the issues facing the Zionist movement did not seem too much to ask. Of course, none of those present knew the kind of determination and single-mindedness that Brandeis had. For the next full day and a half, the delegates sat with Brandeis, answering questions, explaining their various viewpoints, their goals, the backgrounds of some of their leaders. For the first time, Brandeis heard the delegates using Hebrew and Yiddish words that he was not familiar with. He asked them to repeat these words and explain them, and hour after hour he continued to extract every bit of information and understanding that he could from his fellow Zionists.

When the long meeting finally ended, Brandeis felt ready to assume the leadership of the American Zionist movement, and to help it grow and reach out to the many Jews who had, up to that moment, shown almost no interest in the idea of a Jewish homeland in Palestine. Since the world

Zionist movement was forced to remain dormant during the war years, Brandeis must surely have felt that the responsibility for guiding the organization in that critical time rested squarely on his shoulders. He was particularly concerned about the small Jewish community in Palestine.

As Brandeis prepared to lead the Zionist movement, he thought of all the reasons that he had undertaken this new task. He explained years later that he approached Zionism as an American. The problem of the persecuted Jews in the world seemed to him to be very much like the problem of the oppressed industrial workers of America at that time. In other words, here was a case of a wrong that had to be made right. Many prominent American Jews, who had at first stayed away from the Zionist movement, accepted Brandeis's explanation and quickly offered him their support.

As he summed up the great amount of information that he had absorbed in the Zionist emergency meeting, Brandeis realized that he would have to improve the efficiency of the organization in America and attract the financial support of people who still felt uncomfortable about the idea of a Jewish homeland. He also understood that the American Zionist movement would have to be reshaped in an American image. That is, the American Jews who would be called on to help would have to be reached on a very different level from the oppressed, endangered Jews in various European countries for whom Zionism was a personal solution to a very personal problem.

The more Brandeis studied Zionism, the more he began to understand what had motivated him to accept the leadership of the American movement. He told a meeting at this time, "There are two aspects to the Jewish problem— that of the individual Jew and that of the Jews as a collective group. The Jews collectively should enjoy the same right and opportunity to live and develop as do other groups of people. This right of development on the part of the group is essential to the full enjoyment of rights by the individual." Judaism, he preached, was a way of life that should be preserved. And to those Jews who said Jews should assimilate into the larger population and cease being Jewish, his usual response was, "Death is not a solution to the problem of life." The Zionist movement, he taught, aims not only to rebuild the ancient Jewish homeland in Palestine, but also to rebuild the Jewish people and Jewish life wherever Jews live.

But Brandeis, in the fall of 1914, felt that he had little time for theory or philosophy. There was much important work to be done. He began to devote several hours every day to his new Zionist work and quickly put an end to what he considered sloppy, unbusinesslike work methods in the various offices of the movement he now led. He insisted that he receive from all the employees, and from the leaders of the groups that made up the emergency organization, timely written reports on every aspect of their activities.

He sometimes annoyed the volunteers and the paid staff by his demands for reports, but he did not care. The sense of urgency that he felt he now succeeded in imparting to the Zionist movement in America. Although he was always polite and friendly, he could also be tough and demanding, without any hysterics. He tried to show the American Zionist movement that it could be forceful and effective and at the same time efficient and businesslike. He thought that each of the groups within the movement, ranging from the Orthodox Jews to the socialists, should retain its own character, but be ready at all times to unite for the common good.

In 1913, Brandeis had become a member of the Zionist federation. In the fall of 1914, he was named the head of the movement in America, and a year later membership increased dramatically—in some cases by as much as 75 percent. At the 1915 Zionist convention, the delegates agreed to invest $1 million to help develop new industries in Palestine, and Hadassah, the Zionist women's organization, was given funds to send a medical unit to Jerusalem to aid Jews suffering from serious health problems.

Within a few months of taking up his new post, Brandeis moved the Zionist offices from the Lower East Side of New York to uptown addresses. The move indicated that the Zionist movement had become part of the mainstream Jewish community. Three years after he began to lead the Zionists, Brandeis was able to report that the movement now had a list of more than a quarter million people who openly expressed their support for Zionism. This was a very great figure in those days, and one that was later to be cited when the British and Americans debated the question of formally approving the establishment of a Jewish homeland in Palestine.

The number of people who now began to join the various Zionist groups grew, and by 1919 stood at 175,000—compared to about 12,000 five years earlier.

American Jews in 1914 and 1915 followed avidly all the news of the great war raging in Europe. Many of them had relatives who either were serving in various armies or were in great danger because they lived in the path of developing battlefields.

There was also in this period a sense of shock in the American Jewish community, for the daily papers now carried reports of Jewish criminals and Jewish prostitutes in America. For Jews who, in their old homes in Europe, had almost never heard of such things, the reports were demoralizing.

Brandeis earlier had met a leader of the small Jewish community in Palestine, Aaron Aaronsohn, an agricultural scientist who had become famous for having discovered wild wheat in northern Palestine. This was a kind of wheat that scientists had been looking for in order to improve the quality of wheat growing all over the world.

Aaronsohn had made a strong impression on Brandeis, who saw in him a new kind of Jew: a man of the soil, a worker in an industrial plant, a scientist in a laboratory. Like the impoverished Jews of the small villages of eastern Europe, he would be proud, resourceful, intelligent, hard-working—and capable of defending himself against attack.

Perhaps it was Aaronsohn whom Brandeis had in mind when he spoke at a Boston meeting and said, "In the Jewish colonies of Palestine, there are no Jewish criminals." For the American Jews, Brandeis interpreted Zionism as an idealistic movement that would make all Jews proud of their achievements. Zionism, Brandeis preached, would restore to the Jewish people the sense of self-respect they had lost in the last two thousand years.

"Only in Palestine can Jewish life be fully protected from the forces of disintegration," Brandeis wrote. "There alone can the Jewish spirit reach its full and natural development, and by securing for those Jews who wish to settle there the opportunity to do so, not only those Jews, but all other Jews will be benefited, and the long, perplexing Jewish problem will, at last, find solution."

These were troubling days for many American Jews because of the growth of what is usually described as social anti-Semitism. It was undoubtedly a troubling development for Brandeis to observe. In Boston, in August 1910, there had appeared newspaper articles about the desire of Jews from that area to move into certain suburbs where they were not welcome. Real-estate agents in the Boston suburban communities of Roxbury, Dorchester, Brookline, and Brighton simply refused to sell or rent homes or apartments to Jews.

One longtime resident of Roxbury, a Protestant, summed up the feelings of many local people when he wrote that his town began to "fill with precocious Jewish children, all of whom seemed to be taking either piano or violin lessons." A newspaper printed a letter from a reader complaining that "every Jewish junk dealer from Chelsea, every tailor or fur worker in Mattapan wanted his son to become a professional man. And because nearby Harvard was America's oldest and most illustrious university he wanted him to go there and to no lesser place."

In the four decades since Brandeis had enrolled at Harvard, there had developed a changed attitude on the part of many people in Boston, Cambridge, and elsewhere toward Jews. There is little doubt that he was aware of this turn of events, and that it bothered him greatly. It is also quite likely that the changed atmosphere helped to propel him closer to the Jewish community.

In contrast to news reports of Jewish criminals and of anti-Semitic attitudes in the United States, Brandeis recalled his meeting with the young Palestinian Jew, Aaron Aaronsohn. Brandeis had said that "there has developed in Palestine, and there can develop still more in that old land to a higher degree, that spirit of which Mr. Aaronsohn speaks . . . [of] manhood."

Clearly, Brandeis now believed that the Zionist pioneers were the new Puritans.

Between 1914 and 1916, Brandeis devoted the major part of his energies and time to advancing the Zionist cause and to organizing relief and emergency help for Jews both in wartorn Europe and in Palestine. He continued to remain a close and trusted adviser of President Wilson and did not hesitate to use that special relationship to speed the delivery of urgently needed food and medical supplies overseas. America, as a neutral country, could send ships into ports of both sides without too much risk.

Sometimes he must have appeared in that two-year period like a man possessed with a mission who was in a desperate race against time. He continued to speak at all kinds of meetings for the growing Zionist movement, traveling as far west as Portland, Oregon, and wherever a meeting could be organized. He appealed to American Jews to join the movement, and they did so in very large numbers. He also asked for funds to buy food and medicines to aid the Jews in Palestine who had been cut off by the Turks from any contacts with their fellow Jews. Aid was also needed for the tens of thousands of poor Jews who suffered hunger and disease in Russia, Poland, and other places after the battles between the Allies and the Central Powers ended. Millions of dollars were raised and tremendous amounts of supplies were shipped abroad.

Brandeis learned very quickly all the techniques of mass meetings and how to raise funds successfully. In one letter to an official in Chicago, where he was scheduled to speak, he wrote that a big hall should be hired for his appearance, but that it should not be too big. He explained that it is better to have a smaller room be overcrowded and even for some people to be unable to attend than to have a huge hall where there would be many empty seats. He also taught his paid and volunteer staff the importance of announcing large donations before asking for new funds, and was pleased to see the monies so desperately needed begin to come in from people both poor and rich. He insisted on strict, careful records and was pleased to see the number of members, supporters, and donors rise sharply.

His talks around the country generally stressed the same points: The new Zionist movement was a battle for justice for the Jewish people, for basic democratic principles, and for the creation of an ethical society. He never failed to emphasize the nobility of human beings and the brotherhood of man. As he met more and more Jews, men and women who were highly educated as well as those who labored long hours at sewing machines or in factories and stores, he began to have a greater understanding of his people, from whom he had been separated for so long.

He wrote once that "Jews gave to the world its three greatest religions, reverence for law, and the highest con-

Louis, *second from left*, with, *from left*, Nathan Strauss, Stephen Wise, and James Waterman Wise. All four men were
active in the American Zionist movement. KEYSTONE VIEW
COMPANY OF NEW YORK

ceptions of morality. Our teaching of brotherhood and righ-
teousness has, under the name of democracy and social
justice, become the twentieth-century striving of America
and western Europe. Our conception of law is embodied
in the American Constitution, which proclaims this to be a
'government of laws and not of men.' ''

During the two-year period between August 1914 and the
middle of 1916, Brandeis must have spoken at hundreds of
gatherings, appearing before tens of thousands of people.
His leadership, his Lincoln-like image, his message of hope
for the future inspired the American Jewish community.
When he reached the age of sixty, in November 1916, he
was presented with a testimonial scroll signed by ten thousand Jews, all wishing him well and thanking him for his
leadership. Each of the ten thousand people who signed
the birthday scroll also contributed one dollar, thus helping
to raise still more money for their fellow Jews in need.

Somehow, in this same period, he continued to meet with
President Wilson at the White House and to advise him on

various national problems. Brandeis never spoke of the fact that Wilson had yielded to pressure not to appoint him to the cabinet as attorney general. In January 1916, he shared the surprise of the entire country when Wilson announced that he had decided to name him to the Supreme Court, to take the place of Justice Joseph Lamar, who had died.

According to law, Brandeis's nomination was sent to the Senate, where it caused a bombshell. Various names had been mentioned as possible replacements for Lamar, including that of former President Taft. No one had even remotely considered that Brandeis could be a candidate.

A headline in *The Sun*, then a leading New York newspaper, summed up the reactions of most people: First Jew Ever Picked for Bench. Long and Bitter Fight Expected in the Senate Over Confirmation.

# 9

## Supreme Court Justice

*What we must do in America is not to
attack the judges but to educate them.*

For nearly half a year, the judiciary committee of the Senate
investigated every piece of information that could be obtained about Brandeis. Members heard from every enemy
whom Brandeis had ever made in his long career. People
from the railroad and insurance industries said he had acted
in an "unprofessional" manner, and leaders of the American Bar Association said plainly that he was "not a fit person to be a member of the Supreme Court of the United
States." The fact that Brandeis was a Jew certainly influ-
enced the thinking of many people against him.

On the other hand, liberal lawyers and businessmen, as
well as labor leaders, social workers, college professors, and
writers, told the Senate investigators that he was fully qual-
ified, possessing both the highest possible character and the
necessary legal experience.

Finally, in June 1916, the Senate confirmed him by a vote

of 47 to 22. Newspaper headlines in all parts of the country announced that he had won his seat on the Supreme Court. Brandeis's daughter Susan was attending a meeting in New York on the fight for women in America to vote. A woman next to her commented, "I see they confirmed that Jew Brandeis to the Supreme Court." Coldly, Susan replied, "You are speaking to the right person, madam. Mr. Brandeis happens to be my father."

For the next twenty-three years, Brandeis was an outstanding member of the Supreme Court, serving during the administrations of five presidents. Most of his fellow justices were conservative in their understanding of the Constitution and the law, while Brandeis and his old friend from Boston, Oliver Wendell Holmes, Jr., were liberal in their approach.

During the almost quarter of a century that he was on the bench, Brandeis continued to defend the rights of individuals against the possible abuse of power by both government and big business. A free society to him meant that not only did people have the right to their own opinions, but this right was a basic privilege of every American. He wrote in one of his court opinions that "if we would guide by the light of reason, we must let our minds be bold."

Throughout the period of the 1920s and the 1930s, the Supreme Court—often with Holmes and Brandeis dissenting—said that many laws made by various states were unconstitutional when they tried to protect working men and women and to regulate large corporations. Brandeis never wavered in his opinions on the need for such laws and on the need to adapt the laws to the rapidly changing times.

While he was a justice of the Supreme Court, Brandeis wrote more than five hundred opinions. A number of them were at first minority views and were scoffed at but later came to be enacted into law.

While Wilson was in the White House, Brandeis continued to be consulted by him on many vital issues. Wilson once commented that a "talk with Brandeis always sweeps the cobwebs out of one's mind." Brandeis was often called to the White House to discuss issues of the day with the president but never felt too comfortable doing so. He maintained that the executive branch of the government and the judicial branch should be separate and apart.

And sure enough, one day, there came a knock on the door of the Brandeis apartment. It was late in the evening, and Brandeis was in his study, reading and relaxing. When Mrs. Brandeis opened the door, there was President Wilson, smiling and surrounded by his Secret Service bodyguards. He explained that he understood Brandeis's reluctance to visit him in the White House, and so he had come to confer with him at home.

For the son of immigrants from Bohemia who had come to America in search of freedom, a call by the president of the United States at his home was certainly something of a milestone in his life!

From the time he took up his position on the Supreme Court bench in the fall of 1916 until 1921, Brandeis continued to be the major leader of the Zionist movement in America. At home, after a full day as a judge, he would tackle the unending stream of letters and reports that came to him on problems facing the movement in Palestine, in Europe, and in the United States.

Early in 1917, reports began to circulate that the British government, then the strongest worldwide empire, was considering issuing a special statement expressing its support for a Jewish homeland in Palestine. It was electrifying news for Brandeis, who now saw that the dream of the Zionists might soon become a reality. In April 1917, the United States had entered the war against Germany, and Brandeis felt that the time was ripe to push for a Jewish homeland, with the support of the United States. He fully endorsed the idea of the British assuming responsibility for Palestine and expressed his opposition to France or any other country doing so.

In the spring and summer of 1917, Brandeis met a num-

ber of times with the foreign secretary of Britain, Arthur
James Balfour. The two liked each other immensely. They
discussed precise details of the boundaries of Palestine in
which a Jewish homeland would—after the end of the war—
be established. Brandeis also obtained the support of President Wilson for the British declaration and continued to
insist to Balfour that the future Palestine boundaries had
to include the Negev, a desert area, and the Red Sea outlet
to the Indian Ocean.

In November 1917, Britain issued the famous Balfour
Declaration that promised the establishment of a Jewish
homeland in Palestine—an announcement that lifted the
spirits of Jews all over the world. The declaration made Jews
everywhere believe that soon their nearly two-thousand-year-
old dream would become a living reality. For Brandeis, the
Balfour Declaration must have been a moment of great joy.
He could not help wondering also at the strange path his
life had taken—seven years earlier, he had first joined the
Zionists, and now he was the leader of the movement in
America, and the British government had formally and officially promised to help establish a Jewish homeland.

Chaim Weizmann, who was later to become the first
president of Israel and who was the acknowledged leader
of the world Zionist movement, later wrote in his diaries
that it was Brandeis who helped persuade leading Americans, both Jews and non-Jews, to support the British plan.

The Balfour Declaration was only a first step, as far as
Brandeis was concerned. He remained a practical, realistic
man all his life and tried to envision the problems that lay
ahead. At one point, he wrote to Weizmann:

"The utmost vigilance should be exercised to prevent the
acquisition by private persons of land, water rights, or other
natural resources or any concessions for public utilities. These
must all be secured for the whole Jewish people.

"In other ways, as well as this, the possibility of capital-
istic exploitation must be guarded against. The encourage-

ment of all kinds of cooperative enterprises will be indispensable. Our pursuit must be primarily of agriculture in all its branches. The industries and commerce must be incidental as may be required to insure independence and natural development."

As the war in Europe went on, with an Allied victory seen by most people as only a matter of time, Brandeis continued to think of the future. At a meeting of American Zionist leaders in Pittsburgh, held in June 1918, Brandeis outlined his understanding of the future Jewish homeland.

First, he said, there must be political and civil equality for all people, no matter their "race, sex, or faith." Second, "with due respect to existing rights," the Jewish national home should aim for "ownership and control of the whole people of the land, natural resources, and public utilities." Third, all the land should be leased on such conditions that would "insure the fullest opportunity for development and continuity of possession." Fourth, "the cooperative principle should be applied so far as feasible in all agricultural, industrial, commercial and financial undertakings." Fifth, the system of "free public instruction which is to be established should embrace all grades and departments of education."

Many of these basic ideas were eventually adopted by the leaders of Israel when that country was officially founded in 1948.

When World War I finally ended in November 1918, Brandeis made up his mind to see Palestine for himself. In the summer of 1919, while the Supreme Court was in recess for several months, he sailed for Europe and Palestine. A man who enjoyed travel, he still remembered his journeys in Europe when he was a teenager and later visits to Canada and Nova Scotia. Brandeis was as excited about the trip to the Holy Land as a young boy going off on an adventure. He had read so much about Palestine, he knew so much of the past and present, and now he was going to see it all for himself.

In London and Paris, he met for the first time with Weizmann and many of the European Zionist leaders. They talked for long hours about the problems that lay ahead, about the conditions of various Jewish communities in the postwar period, and about the urgent need to raise large sums of money for various purposes.

Brandeis and Weizmann admired and respected each other, but there was a genuine lack of understanding between the two. Weizmann, born in a small town in Poland, where Yiddish was the daily language of most people, had become a respected chemist and a great political leader. With his little beard and accented English, he had won the support of the world's Jews and of many statesmen of the Western world. He had no other interests outside of the Zionist movement and often liked to talk in dramatic terms of future plans and programs.

Brandeis, to Weizmann, must have been a puzzle. He had had no formal Jewish ties until he was over fifty years old, he was a justice of the highest court in the United States, and he was not given to exciting, dramatic statements. Acknowledged to be the leader of American Zionism, Brandeis—who had done so much to enlarge and strengthen the movement in the United States—always wanted to talk of facts and figures, of practical matters.

No one in the top leadership of the Zionist movement doubted Brandeis's devotion or abilities to help the cause, but the European leaders did not know how to talk with him on a one-to-one basis. Somehow, although he was always courteous, he seemed distant, as though he were living on a higher plane than they were. Perhaps it was this trait of standing out in a crowd, of being different from all the other people around him, that made the European leaders uncomfortable with Brandeis. Deep down, much as some of them hated to admit it, the man really seemed to be a kind of prophet who had stepped out of the pages of the Bible.

Troubled by what he considered too much talk and not enough action and clear, practical thinking, Brandeis set off for Palestine. In those days, the trip meant taking a ship from Marseilles, in southern France, to Port Said, in Egypt, and then usually a train across the Sinai to Jerusalem.

When Brandeis and his traveling companion, Jacob de Haas, his old friend from Boston, landed at Port Said, they were startled to be greeted by a band of musicians. The Egyptian Zionists, despite the oppressive July heat in Port Said, had come out to welcome a man they had heard was a great leader of the Jews and a member of the Supreme Court of the United States.

In discussions with British officials who had also come to greet him, Brandeis correctly sensed that, insofar as they were concerned, the Balfour Declaration was a piece of paper which they could ignore if they so chose. He also took a little time out to visit the Egyptian tourist sites, and wrote to his wife, "The most pervading impression [I have] of the East is dreariness . . . but why our lack of beauty and joyousness, which life here is so full of?"

Brandeis who himself was always austere and very conservative in his clothes also seemed to enjoy the colorfulness of the Egyptian women's garments. He complained, in a letter to his wife, about the lack of color and imagination of America's dressmakers and milliners. Presumably he brought home, for his wife and daughters, samples of the Egyptian women's garments he had come to admire.

In a few days, he left for Palestine, his excitement and curiosity at a feverish high.

# 10

# *Palestine*

*It is indeed . . . . a Holy Land.*

Two days after he arrived in Jerusalem, Brandeis wrote to his wife that "it is a wonderful country, a wonderful city." He said that Palestine was a "miniature California, but a California endowed with all the interest which the history of man can contribute and the deepest emotions which can stir a people. The ages-long longing—the love is all explicable now. It has also the great advantage over California of being small.

"The marvelous contrasts of nature," he continued, "are in close juxtaposition. Not only the mind but the eye can grasp them within a single picture. And the marvelous quality of the air brings considerable distances into it. What I saw of California and the Grand Canyon seemed less beautiful than the view from the Mount of Olives upon the Dead Sea and the country beyond.

"And yet all say that northern Palestine is far more beau-

Brandeis, *third from left,* with Professor Henry Friedenwald
in Palestine   ROMAN FREULICH

tiful—and that in this extra-dry season we are seeing the
country at its worst. It was a joy from the moment we
reached it. . . . The way is long, the path difficult, but the
struggle is worthwhile. It is indeed . . . a Holy Land."

During the next sixteen days, Brandeis visited every city
in Palestine and twenty-three of the forty-three settlements
that had been established by 1919. He met with all kinds of
people—farmers, teachers, workers—trying to absorb as
much as possible during his short stay. In a letter to his
wife, he noted that he "did not make speeches in Palestine." Instead, he listened, learned, and stored everything
away in his vast memory.

After his visit, he wrote to his family that "what I have
seen and heard strengthened greatly my conviction that
Palestine can and must become the Jewish homeland as
promised in the Balfour Declaration. The problems and the
difficulties are serious and numerous—even greater than I
had anticipated. But there is none that will not be solved

and overcome by the indomitable spirit of the Jews here and elsewhere."

The nonreligious Jew, Louis D. Brandeis, now began to sound more and more like a biblical prophet. Perhaps if he had known the Talmudic phrase *avira d'ara machkima*, the "air of the Land of Israel makes one wise," he would have understood himself better.

On the trip back home to America, Brandeis had time to think through his visit to Palestine. He remembered the night he spent with Jewish colonists sleeping on the sands of Lydda. He recalled the pro-Arab views expressed to him by the famous British officer, Colonel T. E. Lawrence, who made it clear that he was not in the least supportive of the idea of a Jewish homeland.

Brandeis thought of the different kinds of people he had met in Palestine: the Ashkenazim from eastern and central Europe, the Sephardim from Moslem countries, the fur-hatted Hasidim and the ultra-Orthodox Jews in the Old City of Jerusalem who lived on charity sent from abroad, the radicals and the rabbis, the Yemenite and Bokharan Jews, and the Arab sheiks.

He also recalled his shock at finding that British soldiers stationed in Jerusalem—who had taken control of the country after defeating the Turks—were distributing to visitors copies of a booklet that had first appeared in Russia in 1902, *Protocols of the Elders of Zion*, which claimed a worldwide conspiracy was underway that would lead to the Jews taking over the world. Before taking leave of Europe, he had contacted Balfour, complaining about the quality of the British officials in Palestine and their open anti-Semitic attitude. In the course of time, the British foreign secretary replaced the old officials with people more likely to carry out the provisions of the Balfour Declaration.

Brandeis also considered the Arabs in Palestine, and assumed that they would continue to live in a Jewish homeland, enjoying the benefits of modern agriculture and medicine. In later years he responded to a question on the subject by stating that "Jews lived among the Arabs in perfect amity before and during the war, and I have confidence they will do so again."

The one major problem that disturbed him greatly about Palestine was the prevalence of malaria in the country and the urgent need to drain the swamps to eliminate the dread disease. He felt strongly that a healthful atmosphere free of disease would induce many Jews to come to Palestine, whereas malaria would help to keep them away.

Brandeis was also disturbed by his meetings with Weizmann in Paris, before he sailed for home. (Weizmann was participating in the peace talks in the French capital.) Brandeis had told Weizmann of his strong feelings about ridding Palestine of malaria, and of the need to reshape the world Zionist movement into an efficient organization that would resolve the problems that lay ahead with businesslike approaches. Weizmann wanted to concentrate on political propaganda that would lead to huge migrations of Jews from Europe to the new homeland, whereas Brandeis wanted to clear Palestine of malaria, tackle the problems of soil erosion, and launch the new industries and settlements that would provide the foundation for the future.

There had been bitter arguments between Weizmann and Brandeis, something that the latter had not been accustomed to. He did not change his view that the most important thing that Jews could now do for a Jewish homeland in Palestine was to provide practical, economic support—all the rest, Brandeis was convinced, was merely meaningless talk.

He did not know how to adapt himself to the European methods of meeting and discussing. He enjoyed speaking to the point, citing hard facts and allowing his listeners to decide for themselves what was right and what was not. The Europeans, on the other hand, seemed to him to have a desire to debate endlessly, to ramble, to hold the floor during discussions for hours on end. He found it all too frustrating.

During his long sea journey home, Brandeis reflected on the meeting that Weizmann had had with Emir Feisal, the popular Arab leader, together with Brandeis's close friend, Professor Felix Frankfurter. They had all agreed that the Jews and the Arabs could live together peacefully and that whatever conflicts existed between the two groups were artificially created by British officials.

Brandeis was convinced that the Arab population would benefit from the new science and technology that the Jews would introduce to Palestine and that the Jews also had much to learn from the Arabs. In a letter to an American Zionist leader, he said that "every people has its own character. All peoples give and take, some more and some less, each giving what it has, and if it is wise it takes what it needs. Let us teach all peoples that they are all chosen, and that each has a mission for all."

He returned to the United States more convinced than ever of the prospects of a Jewish homeland becoming a reality in the near future. In the next year, when he again attended a Zionist conference in London and found himself again subjected to long and, to him, fruitless discussions, he told the delegates, "We have come to the time when there are no politics that are valuable except the politics of action." He proposed that non-Zionist Jewish business executives be invited to join an enlarged group that would direct the economic development of Palestine. Many of the old-time Zionist leaders objected; they did not believe that non-Zionists should have a hand in directing the future of the Jewish homeland, no matter how excellent their credentials as business leaders and no matter how noble their motives.

Brandeis was taken aback when Weizmann joined those who opposed his plan, particularly since he had at first supported it. Brandeis announced that he would henceforth no

Brandeis, *middle row, fourth from left,* at World Zionist Congress in London, 1920   ZIONIST ARCHIVES AND LIBRARY

longer be associated with the leadership of the world Zionist movement. He would press his program alone, if need be. He was convinced it was the only sensible way to achieve meaningful results.

By 1921, Brandeis gave up the leadership of the Zionist movement in America, although he never gave up his status as a member of the American organization. He decided instead to find a way outside the world Zionist movement to provide the economic help the Jewish homeland would need.

# 11

## Behind the Scenes

*Duty must be accepted as the
dominant concept in life.*

Throughout the turbulent 1920s, Brandeis, despite his advancing years, became more and more active in those causes that he had devoted his energies to for so long. He could look forward to his seventieth birthday in 1926 with many reasons to be happy with his achievements, but he was never one who liked to look back too much. He always seemed to have so much to do!

He had remained a close adviser and confidant of President Wilson, but during the period of 1921 to 1933, three Republicans occupied the Oval Office in the White House—Warren G. Harding, Calvin Coolidge, and Herbert Hoover—and Brandeis was clearly labeled not only as a liberal but also a fervent supporter of the Democratic party. Therefore his advice was not sought out by these White House incumbents.

During the twelve-year era when the Republicans were in

With his brother, Alfred, *right*, during Louis's last visit to
Louisville, May 1922   ZIONIST ARCHIVES AND LIBRARY

power, Brandeis concentrated his energies in three direc-
tions. Through his loyal friends and supporters who had
left the Zionist leadership when he broke with Weizmann,
he began to build up a new organization that would lay the
groundwork for solid economic development in Palestine.
He also pressed for new laws in Congress that would help
keep America on what he considered a highly moral road,
and, finally, he was anxious to see the emergence of new
leaders of America who would be able to carry on the reform and progressive programs that he strongly favored.

The first program was relatively simple. Working eve-
nings and weekends, as well as during the long summer
recess of the court, he set up the Palestine Economic Corporation (PEC) in which Jewish industrialists—non-Zionists
as well as Zionists—would be enabled to help the future
Jewish homeland with their know-how. Over the years, the
PEC loaned money to struggling new agricultural and industrial enterprises in Palestine; financed the early studies
of the country's chemical and mineral resources, including
those of the Dead Sea; erected industrial buildings where
small manufacturers could lease space at low cost; and car-

ried on a whole series of business efforts—all designed to help make the future Jewish homeland economically viable.

The problem of malaria continued to trouble Brandeis. He remembered his own bout with this disease. He recalled that as a "small boy he had lived in a malarial region, and knew how this disease could hamper and frustrate the efforts of farmers." He learned that the Zionist women's organization, Hadassah, had embarked on a program to provide health care to the Palestinian Jews, and he sent the organization $10,000 to start a cleanup drive against the swamp-induced disease. (He also persuaded Baron Edmond-James Rothschild to contribute $50,000 for the same purpose.) The funds were used in an experimental program near Lake Huleh, in the Galilee, and in one year the epidemic of malaria had been cut almost entirely in that region. Word spread to other Jewish settlements, and they, too, asked for help in ridding themselves of malaria. Within four years of the first drive against malaria, the disease had been virtually eliminated from all of Palestine.

Weizmann and Brandeis, however, still disagreed on basic approaches. Weizmann did not believe that the elimination of malaria was as important as the efforts to revive Hebrew and Jewish culture. As time went on, both leaders drifted more and more apart. Although he held no position of leadership in the American Zionist movement, to many American Jews Brandeis continued to be their Zionist leader.

There were in Palestine at the end of World War I some six hundred thousand Arabs, but the Palestine of the early 1920s included what is today Jordan. For many years, Brandeis believed that all of Palestine—in other words, what is now Israel, the West Bank, and the Gaza Strip—should be included as the Jewish national home. He thought that many Arabs would be happy to sell their land holdings to the Jews and in time move to countries far larger than Palestine, where they would be part of a majority Arab population. He realized, however, that there would always be an

Arab minority in the Jewish homeland, and he felt that this was perfectly acceptable. He compared such a situation with the many minority groups who lived together in the United States, including the Jewish community.

He continued to press ahead with economic programs for the Jewish homeland, and through the Palestine Economic Corporation helped finance a plan to harness the waters of the Jordan River for electric power and land irrigation. The corporation also began to build low-cost housing. Side by side with the PEC, the Palestine Endowment Fund was established to provide for educational and charitable causes, including support for the Hebrew University that had been established on Mt. Scopus in Jerusalem.

Between 1914 and 1921, Brandeis donated more than $170,000 to various Zionist groups; between 1922 and 1939 (when he retired from the Supreme Court), his gifts totaled nearly $450,000. In addition, he sent funds to Henrietta Szold for her work in Hadassah and to his old friend, Jacob de Haas, who had become financially needy. When Brandeis died in 1941, he left an estate of more than $3 million, of which $800,000 was put into trusts for his wife and his two daughters and the remaining amount donated to Hadassah and to the Palestine Endowment Fund.

He had come a long way from the young man who entered Harvard with several hundred dollars borrowed from his brother.

In the midst of all his activities as a Supreme Court justice and as the silent but effective leader of American Jewry's efforts to construct a solid basis for the future homeland, Brandeis continued to press still another program—secretly and privately. He had been too long an activist to be content to sit on the bench in Washington and merely judge. The impulse in him to *do*, to lead in the fight for justice for all people in America, remained strong.

But he was, after all, a member of the highest court in the

land. He had to remain above politics, above anything that could associate him with any particular program, no matter how worthy it was. What Brandeis did, for more than twenty years, has shocked many historians. Almost all of them would agree that his motives were pure, and that he wanted no rewards other than the knowledge that his lifelong mission to improve the well-being of the people of the United States was being carried out. Nonetheless, his secret methods of working remain a problem for many people even decades after his death in 1941.

One of Brandeis's closest friends was a brilliant young man named Felix Frankfurter, a lawyer who became a professor of law at Harvard. Brandeis came to regard him as a "half-brother, half-son." The two shared the same ideas on many issues of the day, including Zionism. Unlike Brandeis, Frankfurter was born abroad, in Vienna, and had come to the United States at a young age. He studied at City College in New York and later at Harvard Law School. For several years, he was an assistant United States attorney, and then worked at the War Department before becoming a Harvard professor. He too later on served as a Supreme Court justice and was a close adviser to President Franklin Roosevelt. He died in 1965.

What Brandeis wanted to do—through Frankfurter—was to see that the social and political reform that he had so fervently fought for would continue. In effect, what Brandeis did was to turn Frankfurter into a private lobbyist for liberal political goals that both men felt were eminently worthwhile and important for the nation. Frankfurter was actually paid for his efforts by Brandeis through a secret bank account, since as a university professor Frankfurter did not have the necessary funds for travel, business entertainment, and other expenses.

The practice, of course, was something that would have been frowned upon if it had been known to the public. A judge, especially a Supreme Court justice, was expected to

Justice Louis D. Brandeis in his Supreme Court robe   ZION-
IST ARCHIVES AND LIBRARY

be beyond such things—he was expected to sit high on his
bench and interpret the law. The fact that other judges en-
gaged in some kind of secret activity does not alter the fact
that Brandeis's actions, from a strictly legal and ethical view,
were questionable. In every way possible, he was extremely
careful about his position. He refused, for example, to accept honorary degrees or to give talks to various groups.

He felt that doing so would rob his office of the dignity that it deserved.

On the other hand, his missionary zeal for a better America would not let him sit back and remain aloof from the problems of the day. In practice, he lived a double life through Frankfurter: As Justice Brandeis, he remained the impartial, fair, and brilliant member of the Supreme Court; at home, in secret correspondence with Frankfurter, he urged a wide variety of programs that he wanted the latter to effect, working in large part through former Harvard students who had taken on important jobs in government.

The double life that Brandeis carried on for nearly a quarter of a century was strange, even dangerous. All of the effort that he put into it was for the same noble causes that he had battled for when he was a young man as the people's attorney. There can be little doubt that he conducted this side of his life with a pang of conscience. And yet he continued to work with Frankfurter secretly for many years because he felt it was the only way that he, Louis D. Brandeis, sitting on the Supreme Court bench, could see improvements in the life of the people for whom he cared deeply.

Life for Justice Brandeis and his wife, Alice, in the middle of the 1920s was pleasant. Although they lived quietly in a Washington apartment during the months that the court was in session, on Sunday afternoons they entertained large numbers of people—generally government officials, visiting dignitaries, law clerks, and Zionist and Jewish leaders. The Brandeis Sunday-afternoon gatherings became very popular occasions for many Washingtonians.

In his personal life, he lived as simply as he could. He continued to use a horse and buggy to get around until the automobiles that had begun to fill the streets made that impossible. The two Brandeis daughters were grown and married and had made the older couple happy and doting grandparents.

Justice and Mrs. Brandeis used a horse and buggy to get around Washington.   ZIONIST ARCHIVES AND LIBRARY

Susan followed her father in becoming an active Zionist and devoted many years to aiding Hadassah. No other members of the Brandeis family followed him into Zionism. The grandchildren spent their summers at the Cape Cod vacation home of the Brandeises, and the warmth and love that Brandeis and his wife demonstrated for each other and for their daughters were also bestowed on the youngsters.

The youngest grandchild, Frank Gilbert, Susan's son, recalls that he and his sister and brother turned out a mimeographed newspaper for the Chatham area, which they called the *Chatham Chatter*. "Grandfather," he recalled recently, "gave us the slogan for the paper—Quality, not quantity."

Not everything, however, was rosy and relaxed. One of Brandeis's colleagues, Justice James C. McReynolds, was openly anti-Semitic. For three years, he would not talk to Brandeis. On one occasion, he wrote to Chief Justice Taft, "As you know, I am not always to be found when there is a Hebrew aboard." Such behavior on the part of a fellow member of the Supreme Court must surely have had an impact on Brandeis.

With the grandchildren in Chatham, Massachusetts, 1935

In this same period, there was a rise of open anti-Semitism in the United States that Brandeis must have regarded with fear and anger. The Ku Klux Klan stepped up its anti-Jewish campaigns, accusing all Jews of being Bolsheviks who wanted to overthrow the government. Henry Ford, whose mechanical and industrial genius had enabled hundreds of thousands of Americans to buy an inexpensive automobile, had financed a Michigan newspaper, the *Dearborn Independent*, that attacked Jews as undesirable aliens. Even Harvard University's president agreed that the number of Jewish students allowed to be enrolled in his school should be limited by quota. For a Harvard alumnus like Brandeis, this must have been particularly painful.

There were, at the time, small but vocal groups of Jews who called for support of the new Soviet government in Russia. Others, who described themselves as anarchists, wanted to see all government controls lifted. The FBI began rounding up suspicious characters. Often anyone who wore a beard, as many Orthodox Jews did, was arrested as a radical.

A kind of hysteria swept America. Although every normally intelligent person knew that the forged and totally false *Protocols of the Elders of Zion*—which had found its way to America—was not worth the paper it was printed on, the head of U.S. Army intelligence in New York claimed that the document proved conclusively that the Russian Revolution was part of a worldwide Jewish conspiracy.

Members of Congress, some government officials, business leaders, and newspapermen began to read an English version of the protocols, which was issued as *The Cause of World Unrest*. Published by George H. Putnam, this vicious attack against Jews claimed that the strategy of the Jews was to "wear out and exhaust the Gentiles [so] that they will be compelled to offer us an international authority, which by its position will enable us to absorb without disturbance all the governmental forces of the world and thus [form] a supergovernment."

Among the business leaders who accepted this nonsense as truth was Henry Ford. His newspaper began to circulate widely and charged "most of the big business, the trusts and the banks, the natural resources and the chief agricultural products, especially tobacco, cotton and sugar, are in control of Jewish financiers or their agents. Jewish journalists are a large and powerful group here. Jews are the largest and most numerous landlords of residence property in the country. They are supreme in the theatrical world. They absolutely control the circulation of publications throughout the country."

Ford's paper attacked Bernard Baruch, the noted financier and White House adviser, and said that presidents Taft and Wilson had been used as "Gentile fronts" for Jewish conspirators. The Federal Reserve System was labeled a "Jewish tool." Even Benedict Arnold was accused of having been a Jewish agent! The Civil War and the assassination of Lincoln were also blamed on Jews.

When one of the leaders of the American Jewish community, Louis Marshall, wrote to Ford, stating that all the charges against Jews in the *Dearborn Independent* were totally false and were the result of hatred and prejudice, one of the paper's executives responded:

"Your rhetoric is that of a Bolshevik orator. These articles shall continue and we hope you will continue to read them and when you have attained a more tolerable state of mind we shall discuss them with you."

Individual Jews and various Jewish groups started lawsuits against Ford. Jewish newspapers urged their readers to stop buying Ford cars. By 1927, Ford auto sales had fallen off by a half-million units; a number of non-Jews joined most Jews in the unofficial boycott. Seven years after launching the paper that spread anti-Jewish hatred and lies, Ford announced that he had been deceived. He claimed he did not know what the paper was publishing and said he wished to make "amends for the wrong done to Jews as fellow-men and brothers, by asking their forgiveness for the harm that I have unintentionally committed." On June 30, 1927, Ford ended his association with the newspaper that had cost him $5 million. It took many years for the Jewish community to forgive and forget and to start buying Ford cars again.

There also developed at this time a new policy, both in government and with the public at large, calling for limiting the number of immigrants who would be allowed to enter the United States. The labor unions opposed wide immigration not only because they feared that it might mean a loss of jobs for their own members, but they claimed that many newcomers to America simply could not be Americanized.

Much of the feeling against free immigration was directed at Jews, most of whom were seeking to enter the United States from Russia and Poland. A Jewish organization survey taken in 1923 showed that about 6½ percent of all those in "almshouses in America" came from Russia and Poland, while more than 26 percent came from Ireland, 20 percent from Germany, and 8 percent from England. The public, however, did not seem to care.

Many resort hotels as well as athletic clubs barred Jews from entering. Many colleges and universities kept a tight quota on the number of Jewish students admitted. Employment ads openly declared "Christians preferred." Certain fields were almost impossible for Jews to enter. One of these was engineering. When Gerard Swope decided he wanted to study electrical engineering at the famous Massachusetts Institute of Technology, he changed his name—it had been Gershon Schwab—and did not admit that he was Jewish. He later went on to become the head of General Electric and one of the great industrialists of America.

The late 1920s were not good years for Brandeis. He sensed that something had gone wrong in America. Often he found himself feeling depressed as he thought about the future of the world, of the United States, and of the Jews.

# 12

## Years of Peril

*There is no hope for those who do not emigrate.*

The worldwide depression that began in 1929 made many people worry about what might happen in the 1930s. In America, millions of people were thrown out of work. The government put up soup kitchens for the hungry; in the big cities, men without jobs stood on street corners, selling apples. Many people lost their homes because they could not pay the mortgages.

In Europe, there had begun to rise a new movement in Germany, Italy, Spain, France, and England that was anti-democratic in spirit and in most cases also anti-Semitic. In Spain and Italy, the followers of this new movement were called Fascists; in Germany, they were known as Nazis. Their ideas were similar to those of the Ku Klux Klan in America. Anti-Semitism for all these groups was an important goal.

Thus, in the early 1930s, Jews in all parts of the world, including those in America, were in many cases suffering

from the effects of the economic depression just like everybody else. In addition, there was a sense of fear and uncertainty among Jews because of the rise of openly anti-Jewish
groups.

In far-off Palestine, an additional serious problem had
arisen for the small Jewish population there—Arab rioting
against Jews had broken out in 1929 and threatened to bring
bloodshed to the Holy Land. Newspapers reported that the
British officials now running the country had allowed the
rioting Arabs to kill and wound Jews and had not allowed
the Jews to defend themselves.

In Hebron, one of the ancient cities of Palestine, a massacre of defenseless Jews that was carried out by Arab mobs
in 1929 sent shock waves around the world.

Justice Brandeis, now in his seventies and beginning to
feel the frailties of old age, looked around him—at America
and at the lands across the seas—and did not like what he
saw. He sensed that a black cloud filled with hatred, despair, and violence had drifted toward the earth and now
threatened all civilization. The Jewish people, especially those
living in Europe, as well as the tiny Jewish community in
Palestine, would soon face a period of great danger. He also
felt that there was not very much he could do to prevent
the threat of evil from engulfing the world.

In 1931, Brandeis celebrated his seventy-fifth birthday.
Many people who admired his work as a Supreme Court
justice joined in wishing him well, as did many Jews around
the world, who looked upon him as an unusually coura-
geous and dedicated Zionist leader and judge.

For fifteen years, Brandeis had served with distinction in
the highest court in the nation, and although he was still
criticized by conservative groups, he had established a reputation as a judge of the people who cared more about people's needs and rights than about legal fine print.

During the depression years, which continued on into
much of the 1930s, most members of the Supreme Court

Louis Brandeis, *right*, and Oliver Wendell Holmes, on Justice Holmes' ninetieth birthday, 1931   ZIONIST ARCHIVES AND LIBRARY

were conservative in their approach to the nation's severe economic problems. Brandeis was one of the outstanding exceptions. In a famous case involving an Oklahoma company, he said that the Supreme Court should set aside its prejudices and stop claiming that new government ideas aimed at ending the economic depression were unconstitutional. In another case, he made it clear that he was against state laws that tried to stop the spread of socialist ideas. Brandeis said that he himself did not share the new ideas of the radicals, but insisted that to him everyone had a right to voice any ideas, no matter how repugnant they might be. The Founding Fathers of America, he reminded his colleagues on the bench, had not been afraid of new ideas.

Although Brandeis became known as a great dissenter, the truth is that of the 528 opinions he expressed during his long term as a justice of the Supreme Court, only 44 were in opposition to the majority. In his personal philosophy, Brandeis always remained a confirmed capitalist. The difference between him and many other justices was simply that he believed strongly that all people, no matter how much he disagreed with them, had a right to express their own viewpoint.

In the world of the 1930s, this was a principle of democracy that was all too often ignored or taken away from the people.

Hopes for a better time in America grew when Franklin D. Roosevelt, a Democrat, was elected president in 1932, assuming office in 1933. In that same year, thoughtful people woke up one morning to discover that a racist by the name of Adolf Hitler, who had campaigned on a platform against the Jews, had succeeded in coming to power in Germany. The name of Hitler's party was the National Socialist Party; its followers were known as Nazis—a word that was to enter the vocabulary of the whole world and come to mean inhuman barbarism.

Hitler's rise to power in Germany, where there was a Jewish community of six hundred thousand, was the first step in the tragedy of the Jewish people in the twentieth century. Before the Nazi regime was crushed in the devastating Second World War that began in 1939 and ended in 1945, millions of soldiers and civilians were killed. Among them were 6 million Jews, one-third of the world's Jewish community, who had been singled out for mass murder. This planned massacre of the Jews, known now as the Holocaust, did have one positive result—it helped spur on the Zionist movement's programs to create a Jewish homeland where Jews could be secure. Three years after the end of World War II, the State of Israel was proclaimed.

In the midst of the depression years, American Jews had been forced to turn their attention to their own problems, away from Palestine and from their fellow Jews in Europe. It was, in the early 1930s, a time when Jewish doctors, dentists, and lawyers were happy to find work as waiters; Jews who had succeeded in getting teachers' licenses were now cabdrivers; storekeepers and home owners lost their possessions. Jews in cities across the country found themselves asking Jewish organizations for help. Many Jews of that time were too ashamed to ask for relief aid from the government; applying to their own Jewish groups for help was less embarrassing for them. In 1932, in Minneapolis, for example, the number of Jews who applied to the local Jewish agency for emergency funds, for food and rent money, grew by 100 percent.

Many Jewish newspapers offered free space to people looking for jobs or offering jobs—but there were few jobs offered.

The depression did not do too much damage to the very rich segments of the population. Hungry people waiting in line at soup kitchens watched with amazement as millionaires pulled up to fancy hotels in chauffeur-driven limousines for expensive dinners. Bitterness and despair were in the air of America.

The election of Roosevelt as president was the first step in what many people hoped would be a national recovery. The American Jews voted for him in overwhelming numbers; one Jewish magazine described him as a "friend of the oppressed." When Roosevelt ran for reelection in 1936, after having launched a series of economic steps meant to end the depression, he received huge Jewish support. In one section of Chicago, for example, 96 percent of the Jews voted for him. He became the symbol of the Jews' hope—for America, and for the Jewish people who looked around them and saw that in many parts of the world hatred for Jews and violence against them continued to expand.

The enthusiastic response of American Jews to the Zionist movement that had been created by Brandeis's leadership weakened sharply in the 1930s. In 1933, the Zionist Organization of America reported a total membership of thirteen thousand. A year's membership was six dollars—the amount needed to feed a family of four for a week. Membership continued to drop as the depression remained, even when dues were cut to three dollars. In 1935, the once proud organization that had numbered tens of thousands of American Jews had a paid membership of eighty-eight hundred.

The Arab riots in Palestine had resulted in a decision by the British officials to reexamine their programs. Various commissions went to investigate, and in 1930 the British government announced that the best solution to the problems growing between the Jews and Arabs was to stop any further Jewish immigration. The study group claimed that there simply was not enough usable land for farming and insisted that Palestine had to remain primarily a small agricultural nation.

The Zionist leaders believed strongly that they could turn long-neglected arid land into productive farming and residential areas through the use of the latest scientific developments. They insisted they would be able to make the desert bloom again—as it had in biblical times.

One of the British investigative groups announced that

Brandeis in the early 1930s   ZIONIST ARCHIVES AND LIBRARY

no more land should be sold to Jews, and that all immigration should be halted until such time as everyone in Palestine was holding down a job.

Protests against the plan came from many quarters. Even the great Zionist leader, Chaim Weizmann, who had for so many years continued to press for a Jewish homeland and had allowed nothing to discourage him, was filled with despair. He was quoted as saying, after he read the British recommendations: "Never can there be a Jewish state . . . I no longer believe in the Jewish state. It can never be."

Brandeis, on the other hand, refused to be depressed. He used every contact that he had ever made with British officials to help defeat the recommendations. He encouraged a demonstration against the British for their betrayal of the Balfour Declaration. This brought together fifty thousand Jews at the old Madison Square Garden in New York, more than half of whom were forced to remain outside for lack of room. By 1931, the British prime minister, Ramsay Mac-Donald, announced that the earlier statement about limiting land sales to Jews and immigration to Palestine was no longer in effect. The British leader's announcement restored the confidence of Jews in the Balfour Declaration. A crisis had come and gone. Only a small number of people were aware of the role that Brandeis had played in saving the day.

Although many people, Jews included, did not take Hitler's threats against the Jewish people seriously, Brandeis did. Soon after the Nazi dictator took over the leadership of Germany, he began a series of actions against its Jewish population. From 1933 to 1935, most people were concentrating on the basic problem of providing enough food to feed their families. Many people believed, probably because they wished it to be so, that Hitler's earlier rantings against the Jews would come to an end when he became a responsible government official. It was a case of wishful thinking at its worst.

As early as April 1933, Brandeis was already deeply concerned about the future of Europe's Jews, particularly those in Germany. He urged his close friend Felix Frankfurter, who was well known to President Roosevelt, to intercede on their behalf. Probably what was needed, Brandeis thought, was a strong statement by the president against the Nazis' persecution of the Jews. In addition, America should open its doors to absorb the German Jews as immigrants, a step that he surely realized would not be easy in view of the terrible economic situation in America.

Every day seemed to bring more bad news for the Jews of Germany. Steadily, their rights were being taken away from them, as well as their chance to earn a living. Rabbi Stephen Wise, one of Brandeis's closest friends, had toured Europe, talking to knowledgeable people. He brought back a report that had a profound effect on Brandeis. Wise said that it was urgent to rescue the Jews from Germany, and that the best solution was to bring them to Palestine. The Nazis meant what they said, the rabbi warned.

In 1936, new Arab riots broke out in Palestine against the Jews. Many were killed and wounded. The British government once again said that it would stop all Jewish immigration to Palestine—this at a time when more than ever the Jews of Germany desperately needed a safe haven. Brandeis was convinced that the emigration of the German Jews was a matter of urgency. He warned that "there is no hope for those who do not emigrate."

An old friend of Roosevelt, Wise managed to persuade the president to use his influence with the British to withhold any announcement about stopping Jewish immigration to Palestine. The British accepted Roosevelt's suggestion, and immigration was not banned. A year later, however, there was still another British group that went to investigate the troubles in Palestine. Viscount Peel was the chairman of the group, known as the Peel Commission.

To everyone's surprise, the Peel group blamed Britain for its handling of the Palestine question. Britain had promised both the Jews and the Arabs the same thing in Palestine, and that was the main cause of all the rioting and trouble. The solution, Peel said, was to divide Palestine—the area west of the Jordan river, which includes Israel today, the West Bank, and the Gaza district—into three separate areas: a Jewish state of approximately 1,550 square miles, with its western boundary on the Mediterranean; a larger section for an Arab state that would include the eastern region of Palestine; and a "neutral" zone that would include Jerusalem and Bethlehem and be controlled by Britain. The vast Negev Desert and half of the West Bank would go to the Arabs.

Nobody liked the idea. The Arabs denounced it, and the Jews said they could not conceive of a Jewish homeland without Jerusalem. They also opposed the transfer of the

Negev to the Arabs. Brandeis thought the plan was all wrong, not so much because it cut off the Jews from areas that had been part of biblical Israel, but mostly because he believed such a small area simply could not succeed economically. What also troubled him was the breaking of a promise—the Balfour Declaration, he felt, had been abandoned by the British. He called the Peel report an "ignoble, stupid action."

Brandeis was not surprised that Weizmann supported the plan. The world Zionist leader said that it was not the best solution to the problem, but it was better than nothing. Brandeis turned for support of his view to the militant young leader from Palestine, David Ben-Gurion, for whom he had great respect. They had been meeting together for a number of years, discussing economic and other projects in Palestine. Brandeis had concluded that the Palestinian was a fighter, willing to take a stand on a given issue, no matter how unpopular it might be.

Brandeis had donated thousands of dollars to Ben-Gurion, to use in Palestine in any way he saw fit. By 1936, a close bond had developed between the two men—the tall, soft-spoken justice and the short, stocky Palestinian, who spoke English with a peculiar mixture of British and Polish accents. (Ben-Gurion, who was to become Israel's first prime minister, was born in Poland.) When Ben-Gurion told Brandeis in 1936, after a new outbreak of Arab rioting, that the self-defense organization set up by the Jews in Palestine, the Haganah, was unable to function properly because of a lack of arms, the Supreme Court justice did not hesitate. From his own funds, he turned over $40,000 to him, so that the Haganah could obtain arms and defend the Jews in Palestine.

Brandeis felt betrayed when he was informed that Ben-Gurion also supported the Peel plan. The two met in the summer of 1937; Ben-Gurion felt the need to explain his position to his old friend and supporter. The Palestinian leader agreed that the area proposed by Peel was small, and that it was a betrayal of the Balfour Declaration by Britain, but insisted that there was no alternative—and that it was better to have a tiny Jewish state than to continue to suffer under British rule.

The hours-long discussion between the two, which took place in the peaceful setting of Chatham on Cape Cod, was almost like a battle between two great lawyers arguing before an invisible jury. Brandeis reminded Ben-Gurion that the great Herzl had also been mistaken when he, at one time, was ready to accept a Jewish national home in Uganda, in East Africa, offered to him by the British. Brandeis said he did not like to disagree with Ben-Gurion who, after all, was living in Palestine, coping with the problems there on a daily basis.

On the other hand, Brandeis continued, his being far away in America gave him a more long-range view, and he was convinced that accepting the Peel offer was a major blunder for the future. As things turned out, neither convinced the other. Nothing further came of the Peel plan, which the British themselves ignored.

The problems of the Jews in Europe continued meanwhile to grow worse. By 1938, Germany had united with Austria, and soon all of the Jews of Germany, Austria, and later Czechoslovakia, were in grave danger. A feeling that war might break out soon descended on the whole world. The Germans, under the new Nazi regime, had defied everybody and had been arming themselves heavily. The questions of Jewish rescue and emigration, and the transfer of Jews to Palestine, were now the principal sources of worry for Brandeis and for all thoughtful Jewish leaders. The lives of hundreds of thousands of people were at stake.

Early in 1939, the British started to arm themselves, fearing a Nazi attack. Palestine was of no great importance to them. In February of 1939, fearing new limits on Jewish immigration to Palestine, Brandeis wrote to the British prime minister, Neville Chamberlain:

"I cannot believe that your government has fully considered how shattered would be the faith of the people of this troubled world in the solemn undertakings of even democratic governments if Great Britain so drastically departed from her declared policy in reference to the Jewish National Home. I urge you to consider the cruel plight of the Jews in the world today and not to crush their most cherished and sanctified hopes."

The British ambassador in Washington, on behalf of Chamberlain, wrote to Brandeis, saying his views would be given every consideration. Brandeis was too experienced in diplomacy not to know that such a response was meaningless. A few days later, he called on President Roosevelt at the White House.

Roosevelt had a great deal of respect and affection for Brandeis, whom he frequently referred to as Isaiah and as a grand old man. Roosevelt had told many American Jewish leaders how sympathetic he was to the situation of the Jews, and how much he supported the idea of a Jewish national home in Palestine. But he had also admitted that there were limits to what he could do.

Sitting in the Oval Office, Brandeis told Roosevelt of Chamberlain's response. He described the desperate plight of thousands of foreign-born Jews who had been driven by the Nazis to the Polish border and were not allowed to enter Poland. They were living in a no-man's-land, and their hope was all but gone. He asked Roosevelt to speak out on behalf of free Jewish immigration to Palestine, and to press the British to live up to the intent of the Balfour Declaration that had been approved by the United States and other democracies.

Roosevelt expressed sympathy with Brandeis but said he did not think there was much he could do. The two men had been close for many years, the president often consulting Brandeis on various efforts to bring about economic recovery in America. A few weeks earlier, following a mild heart attack, Brandeis had retired from the Supreme Court.

Now, a terrible fear for the future of the Jews of Europe would not let him rest. He looked across the desk at Roosevelt, perhaps trying to convince him that the Germans were about to unleash a terrible war against the free world and against the Jews in particular.

But Brandeis was also a realist. He knew that Roosevelt was a master politician, and that he could not feel the same anguish in his heart that Brandeis felt for his fellow Jews. The two parted on a cordial note. Deep in his heart, Brandeis felt that never before in Jewish history had there been such an impending tragedy as the one that now seemed so clear to him.

As he left the White House for his waiting car, Brandeis consoled himself with the knowledge and faith that somehow, at some time, in spite of everything, the Jews would once again have a homeland of their own. Then they would be safe from the threat of a new Hitler.

In May of 1939, the British issued a white paper on Palestine. A total of seventy-five thousand Jews would be allowed to enter Palestine in the next five years. After that, Jewish immigration would come to an end. Chamberlain had in effect canceled the Balfour Declaration.

When the white paper was made public, the phone in the Brandeis apartment in Washington did not stop ringing. From all over the country, Jewish leaders wanted to know what he thought could or should be done. Now in his eighty-third year, Brandeis did not like talking on the phone. He spoke with his callers through one of his former law clerks. To all who called, he could only say, "Where will a poor Jew go now?" A few weeks later, he sent a statement to the Zionist organization. It was in the form of a question: "What does the world propose to do with the Jews for whom exile is enforced?" At that time, nobody had an answer.

Age had begun to creep up on Brandeis. He could no longer row but still enjoyed sitting in a canoe or rowboat and being taken for a peaceful ride. Once, when he returned home, he found the elevator in his apartment house not working. He did not know how to climb five floors without possibly harming his frail health. His wife, aware of the situation, had called one of his former clerks for help. The clerk and the janitor of the building, a husky black man, sat Brandeis in a chair. He continued to wear his coat and hat as the two men lifted him in the chair and carried him up the five flights. He remained quiet throughout the unusual trip, looking straight ahead. Mrs. Brandeis had, in the meanwhile, rushed downstairs to make sure all went well— and the two men, after catching their breath, had to carry her up as well.

For many years, the Brandeises had entertained leading Washington personalities at their apartment. Among those who came frequently were Senator Harry Truman, later to become president, and Dean Acheson, a one-time law clerk of the justice who later became secretary of state.

One visitor recalled that the tea was weak and each guest received only one cookie, but the talk was superb. Brandeis would sit in his chair, and Mrs. Brandeis would bring over a visitor, and the two would talk about the problems of the day. Brandeis often wanted to know about his guest's activities and how they affected the country as a whole. One day, one of the guests who came was an American diplomat stationed in the Soviet Union, which had only recently been recognized by the United States. Brandeis asked him the question, "How many tons of cotton were produced in Turkestan last year?" His visitor had no idea, and Brandeis quickly motioned to his wife to bring someone else over— he did not have time to waste on people who did not know what he considered basic information.

In the summer of 1939, Brandeis and his wife returned to Cape Cod, where their simple home in Chatham had given them so many happy years. He could often be seen walking along the beach, dressed in a sloppy old sweater, deep in thought. His children and grandchildren stayed with the older couple for much of the summer, and there were memorable days for them all.

In those peaceful summer months before World War II broke out in Europe on September 1, when the German army invaded Poland, Brandeis must certainly have been thinking about the events of November 9, 1938, in Germany and Austria. That night, known as *Kristallnacht*, or Night of Crystal Glass, thousands of Jewish homes and stores, synagogues and Jewish organizations, were attacked and burned to the ground, and thousands of Jews were arrested and sent to concentration camps.

He remembered what the former governor of New York, Al Smith, who had tried to become president, had said at the time: "The German people are incapable of living under a democratic government." He also recalled what a dynamic young lawyer in New York, Thomas E. Dewey, who ran for president later, had commented: "The civilized world stands revolted by the blood pogrom against a defenseless people, by a nation run by madmen."

Brandeis also thought about Roosevelt's reaction to the attacks on the Jews in the night of murder, arson, and arrests. The president had said he was "deeply shocked" by what had happened, and he had also instructed the American ambassador to leave Berlin at once as a sign of displeasure. But had it been enough? Had not the United States become one of the greatest bulwarks of freedom in the world? Could the president have banned the import of all German goods? Would that have stopped the Nazis?

Brandeis continued to have the troubling feeling that with very few exceptions, only the Jews seemed to care about the fate of the Jews. It was disturbing to him also to know that American supporters of Nazi Germany were openly showing their contempt for Jews and for democratic institutions. He found it hard to accept that the people who had produced a Goethe were now pressing for a Nazi world.

Alice and Louis in a relaxed moment   ZIONIST ARCHIVES AND
LIBRARY

He found himself, during those walks on the Cape Cod
sands, thinking about his own role in the last few years.
Had he done enough for the Jewish national home? Could
he have done more to persuade the leaders of America and
England to throw open their doors to endangered Jews? He
was no longer a young man, and his health had in recent
months begun to fade. Being a realist, he knew that he did
not have that much time left.

He found himself remembering something his old friend,
Harold Ickes, the secretary of the interior, a non-Jew, had
told him at the end of 1938 following the *Kristallnacht* attacks. In blunt language, for which he was well known, Ickes
had told Brandeis:

"I would like to get two or three hundred of the rich Jews
of America together in a room and tell them that they
couldn't hope to save their money by meekly accepting

whatever humiliations others chose to impose on them."
Ickes had told him in strong tones that the Jews should be-
come more aggressive in defending the Jews, just as the
Catholics were.

Brandeis remembered what he had replied—that there
were certain rich Jews, most of them of German origin, who
were cowards. He had agreed with Ickes about the terrible
situation of the Jews, and they both expressed contempt for
these cowardly Jews.

On the other hand, Brandeis argued with himself, then
why didn't he, a respected leader in America, call together
such a meeting? Could he in good conscience hide behind
the excuse that he was a sick old man?

It was a summer of thinking—of the past, the present,
and the future. Always a stickler for precise information,
Brandeis knew that despite the urgent need for German Jews
to find refuge from the Nazi threat, the number of Jews
admitted to the United States in 1933 was only 2,372. In
1934, the number had risen to 4,137, and a year later the
total reached 4,837.

There had been a sharp cut in all immigration to the United
States since 1930. Labor unions, even those with large Jewish memberships, had approved these restrictions. Brandeis
recalled a survey taken a few months earlier by *Fortune*
magazine. While 94 percent of the American people said
they condemned the Nazis' behavior toward the Jews in the
November 1938 *Kristallnacht* attacks, 83 percent opposed any
changes in the immigration laws that might allow Jewish
refugees to enter the United States.

The events of the ship *St. Louis* still haunted all American
Jews in that summer of 1939. A German vessel out of Ham-
burg, the *St. Louis* sailed in May for Cuba with more than
900 Jewish men, women, and children who held visas for
that island nation. When the ship reached Havana, the Cu-
ban authorities allowed no one to land, announcing that the
visas were frauds and worthless. Cuba is located only ninety

miles from the United States, and the Jewish refugees on board cast their eyes toward America, hoping that they would be admitted.

The American Jewish community seemed to be paralyzed or afraid to speak up on behalf of the Jews on the ship. Even the usually outspoken leaders like Rabbi Wise were publicly silent. They would have welcomed an outcry from the non-Jewish community of America, demanding that the ship be allowed to land at an American port, but no such outcry ever came. The humane German captain of the vessel, after sailing slowly along the eastern seaboard of the United States, reluctantly headed back to Europe. The doors of America remained shut. The passengers were permitted to disembark in England, France, and Holland. Most of those who were temporarily saved in June of 1939 perished in the Nazi death camps a few years later.

In September 1939, German armies attacked Poland. Within days, there were thousands of casualties. The Germans had signed a peace treaty with the Soviet Union and so felt free to destroy Poland before they turned toward the west. By the summer of 1940, they had defeated France, Norway, Denmark, Belgium, and Holland. They were allied with Italy, and Spain was friendly although neutral. Romania and Hungary were also friendly to the Nazis. The Nazis continued to fight the war in Greece, Yugoslavia, and North Africa while their ally in the Pacific, Japan, successfully attacked British positions in the Far East. In 1940, only England continued to fight against the Nazis. Until December 1941, the United States was officially neutral, although America had begun to provide England with arms and supplies.

It was a bleak period for the free world. For Jews, it was a moment of deep darkness. Wherever they went, the Nazis singled out the Jews for brutal treatment in concentration camps and eventual massacre. Not given to public displays of emotion, Brandeis must in this period have been choked up with bitter tears. Zionist friends had told him that the Jews of Palestine, fearful of a Nazi sweep through North Africa which would end up in the Holy Land, had prepared to commit suicide rather than submit to Nazi butchery.

But God was good to Brandeis. On October 5, 1941, two months before the Japanese attacked Pearl Harbor and America entered the war, he died after a brief illness. He was a month short of eighty-five years of age. He did not live to see his beloved country fighting an all-out war in Europe, North Africa, and the Pacific. Had he lived another year, he would have been unable to believe the horrible truth about the Nazis' plan for the massacre of Jews, which became widely known in December 1942.

On the other hand, he did not live to see the establishment of Israel in 1948, an event that would have given him so much joy.

# 13

# *A Great American*

*There is in most Americans some spark of
idealism, which can be fanned into a flame.*

In December 1942, one year after Brandeis died, a memorial
meeting took place in Washington at which leading judges
and lawyers spoke, honoring the contributions of Justice
Brandeis to America. One of those who spoke at the memorial was Francis Biddle, a judge who also served as attorney general of the United States from 1941 to 1945.
Biddle said:

"Brandeis quietly dedicated his life to the service of his
country. To be sure, he was too fundamentally simple to
think of anything he did as a dedication. But as much as
anyone I have ever known, he was innately selfless. Nor
was it the selflessness of a man who held off the world—
Brandeis lived intensely in his world, a world where the
economic struggle for power, the wretched inequalities between comfort and suffering, the failure of the accepted
democratic processes to give scope to the needs of a new
industrial era enlisted his heart as well as his mind.

"He believed profoundly that behind every argument is someone's ignorance, and that disputes generally arise from misunderstanding. Mr. Brandeis's thought was always of man, as when he said in 1914: 'We must bear in mind all the time that however much we may desire material improvement and must desire it for the comfort of the individual, the United States is a democracy and that we must have, above all things, men. It is the development of manhood to which any industrial and social system should be directed.'

"That was the chief reason why he was so deeply concerned with the growth of huge corporations as presenting a grave danger to American democracy. Brandeis believed that every man in this country should have an actual opportunity, and not only what he termed a paper opportunity. The social justice for which we are striving was for him not an end but a necessary incident of our democracy. The end is the development of the people by self-government in the fullest sense, which involves industrial as well as political democracy.

"Brandeis takes his place in the moving stream of history as a great American whose life work brought nearer to fulfillment the essentially American belief in equality of opportunity and individual freedom—the dream that Jefferson, whom Brandeis referred to as the first civilized American, had cherished, and Lincoln, sprung from such different roots. Brandeis is in their tradition, the American tradition of those who affirm the integrity of men and women."

# INDEX

Page numbers in *italics* refer to captions.